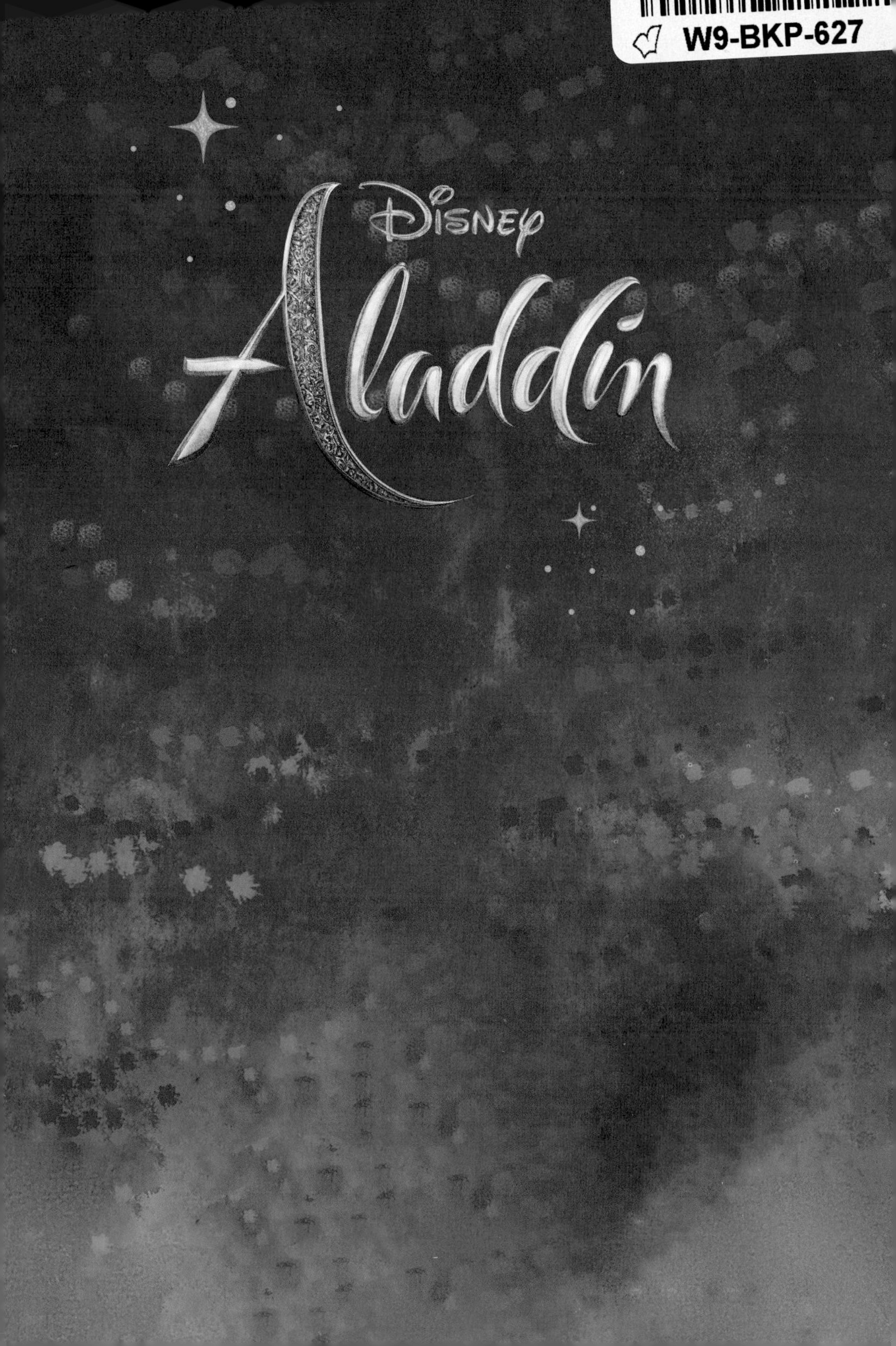
Disney
Aladdin

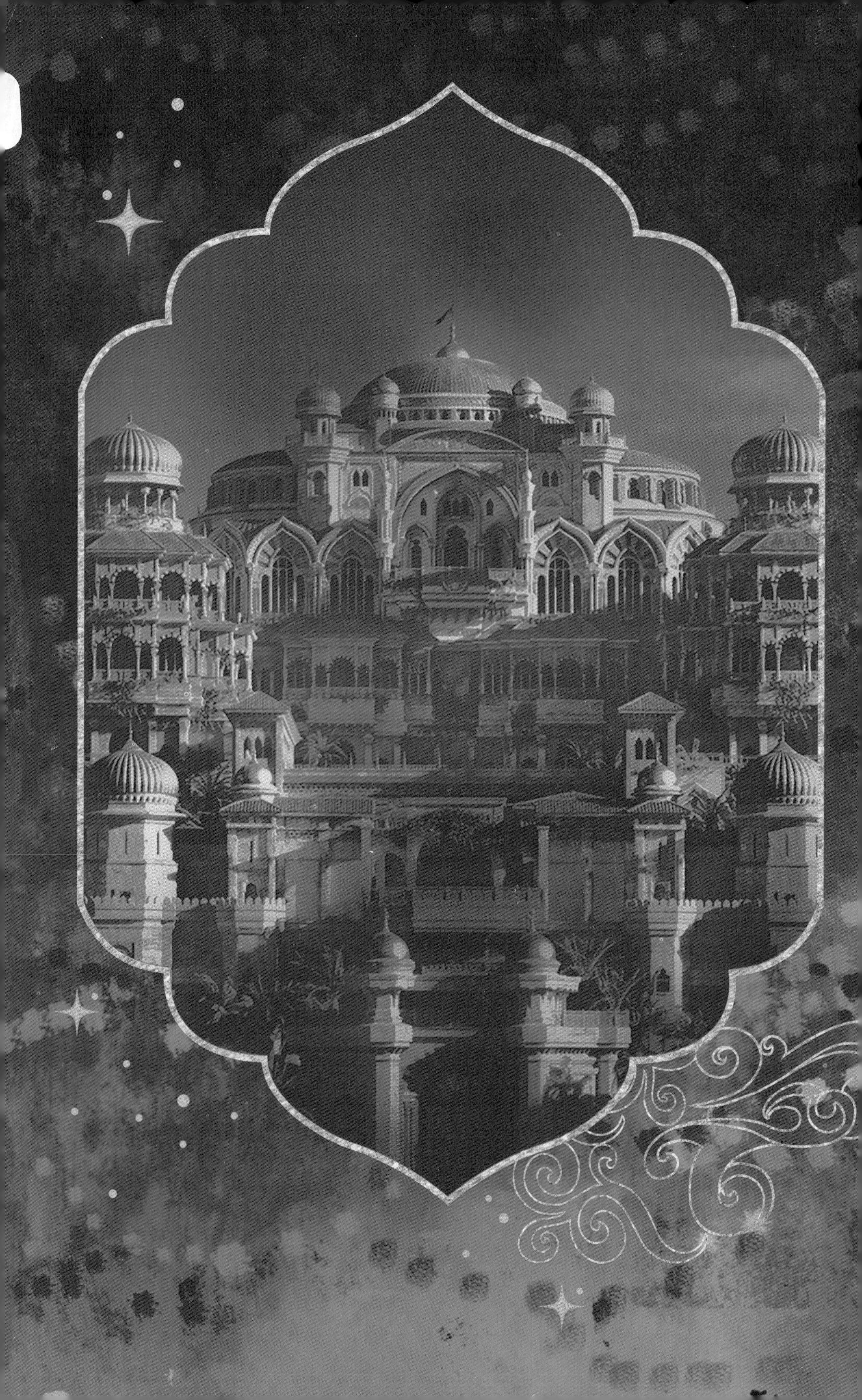

DISNEP Aladdin

Four Tales of Agrabah

Script
Corinna Bechko

Art
Pablo Andrés
Lalit Kumar Sharma
Diego Pérez Galindo

Colors **Jordi Escuin Llorach**
and **DC Alonso**

Lettering **Richard Starkings**
and **Comicraft's Jimmy Betancourt**

Cover Art **Pablo Andrés**
and **Jordi Escuin Llorach**

Dark Horse Books

Dark Horse Books
President and Publisher Mike Richardson
Editors Freddye Miller and Shantel LaRocque
Assistant Editors Judy Khuu and Brett Israel
Designer Anita Magaña
Digital Art Technicians Christianne Gillenardo-Goudreau, Allyson Haller, and Josie Christensen

Neil Hankerson, *Executive Vice President* • Tom Weddle, *Chief Financial Officer* • Randy Stradley, *Vice President of Publishing* • Nick McWhorter, *Chief Business Development Officer* • Dale LaFountain, *Chief Information Officer* • Matt Parkinson, *Vice President of Marketing* • Cara Niece, *Vice President of Production and Scheduling* • Mark Bernardi, *Vice President of Book Trade and Digital Sales* • Ken Lizzi, *General Counsel* • Dave Marshall, *Editor in Chief* • Davey Estrada, *Editorial Director* • Chris Warner, *Senior Books Editor* • Cary Grazzini, *Director of Specialty Projects* • Lia Ribacchi, *Art Director* • Vanessa Todd-Holmes, *Director of Print Purchasing* • Matt Dryer, *Director of Digital Art and Prepress* • Michael Gombos, *Senior Director of Licensed Publications* • Kari Yadro, *Director of Custom Programs* • Kari Torson, *Director of International Licensing* • Sean Brice, *Director of Trade Sales*

Disney Publishing Worldwide Global Magazines, Comics And Partworks
Publisher Lynn Waggoner • *Editorial Team* Bianca Coletti (*Director, Magazines*), Guido Frazzini (*Director, Comics*), Carlotta Quattrocolo (*Executive Editor*), Stefano Ambrosio (*Executive Editor, New IP*), Camilla Vedove (*Senior Manager, Editorial Development*), Behnoosh Khalili (*Senior Editor*), Julie Dorris (*Senior Editor*), Mina Riazi (*Assistant Editor*), Jonathan Manning (*Assistant Editor*) • *Design* Enrico Soave (*Senior Designer*) • *Art* Ken Shue (*VP, Global Art*), Manny Mederos (*Senior Illustration Manager, Comics and Magazines*), Roberto Santillo (*Creative Director*), Marco Ghiglione (*Creative Manager*), Stefano Attardi (*Computer Art Designer*) • *Portfolio Management* Olivia Ciancarelli (*Director*) • *Business & Marketing* Mariantonietta Galla (*Marketing Manager*), Virpi Korhonen (*Editorial Manager*)

Names: Bechko, Corinna, 1973- author. | Vite, Pablo, artist, cover artist. |
    Sharma, Lalit (Lalit Kumar), artist. | Galindo, Diego, 1978- artist. |
    Llorach, Jordi Escuin, cover artist.
Title: Disney Aladdin : four tales of Agrabah / script, Corinna Bechko ; art,
    Pablo Vite, Lalit Kumar Sharma, Diego Perez Galindo ; colors, Jordi
    Escuin Llorach, David de la Cal Alonso ; lettering, Richard Starkings and
    Comicraft's Jimmy Betancourt ; cover art, Pablo Vite with Jordi Escuin
    Llorach.
Other titles: Four tales of Agrabah | Aladdin (Motion picture : 2019)
Description: First edition. | Milwaukie, OR : Dark Horse Books, 2019.
Identifiers: LCCN 2019001346 | ISBN 9781506712673 (paperback)
Subjects: LCSH: Graphic novels. | BISAC: JUVENILE FICTION / Comics & Graphic
    Novels / Media Tie-In. | JUVENILE FICTION / Fairy Tales & Folklore /
    General. | JUVENILE FICTION / Classics.
Classification: LCC PZ7.7.B425 Dis 2019 | DDC [Fic]--dc23
LC record available at https://lccn.loc.gov/2019001346

Published by Dark Horse Books, A division of Dark Horse Comics LLC
10956 SE Main Street, Milwaukie, OR 97222
DarkHorse.com
To find a comics shop in your area, visit comicshoplocator.com

First edition: May 2019
ISBN 978-1-50671-267-3
Digital ISBN 978-1-50671-284-0
10 9 8 7 6 5 4 3 2 1
Printed in the United States of America

Come explore the wondrous city of Agrabah—full of color, liveliness, and excitement! Walk through the beautiful streets and meet people from all walks of life, from locals to royalty!

Embark on the early journeys of the characters fated to meet! Take a glimpse into the life of Aladdin during his time as a vagabond living on the streets of Agrabah. Then, enter the Sultan's Palace and gaze into the imagination and dreams of young Princess Jasmine as she immerses herself in a world of everlasting knowledge. Return to present day and let Magic Carpet, Abu, and Raja take you on a ride that's anything but monkey business! Finally, reveal a tale of one of Genie's first appearances out of the magic lamp!

A whole new world awaits in the lustrous city of Agrabah…

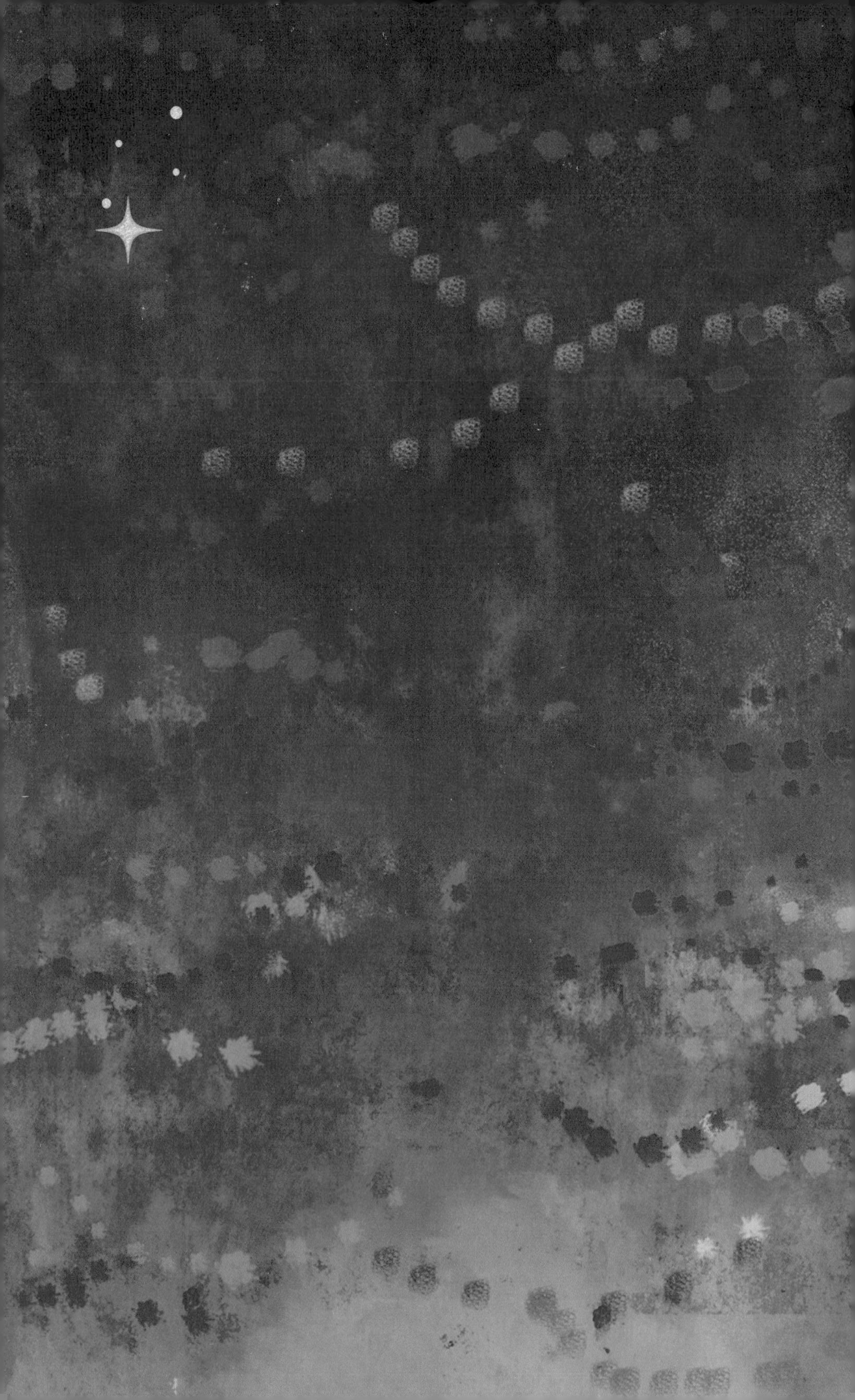

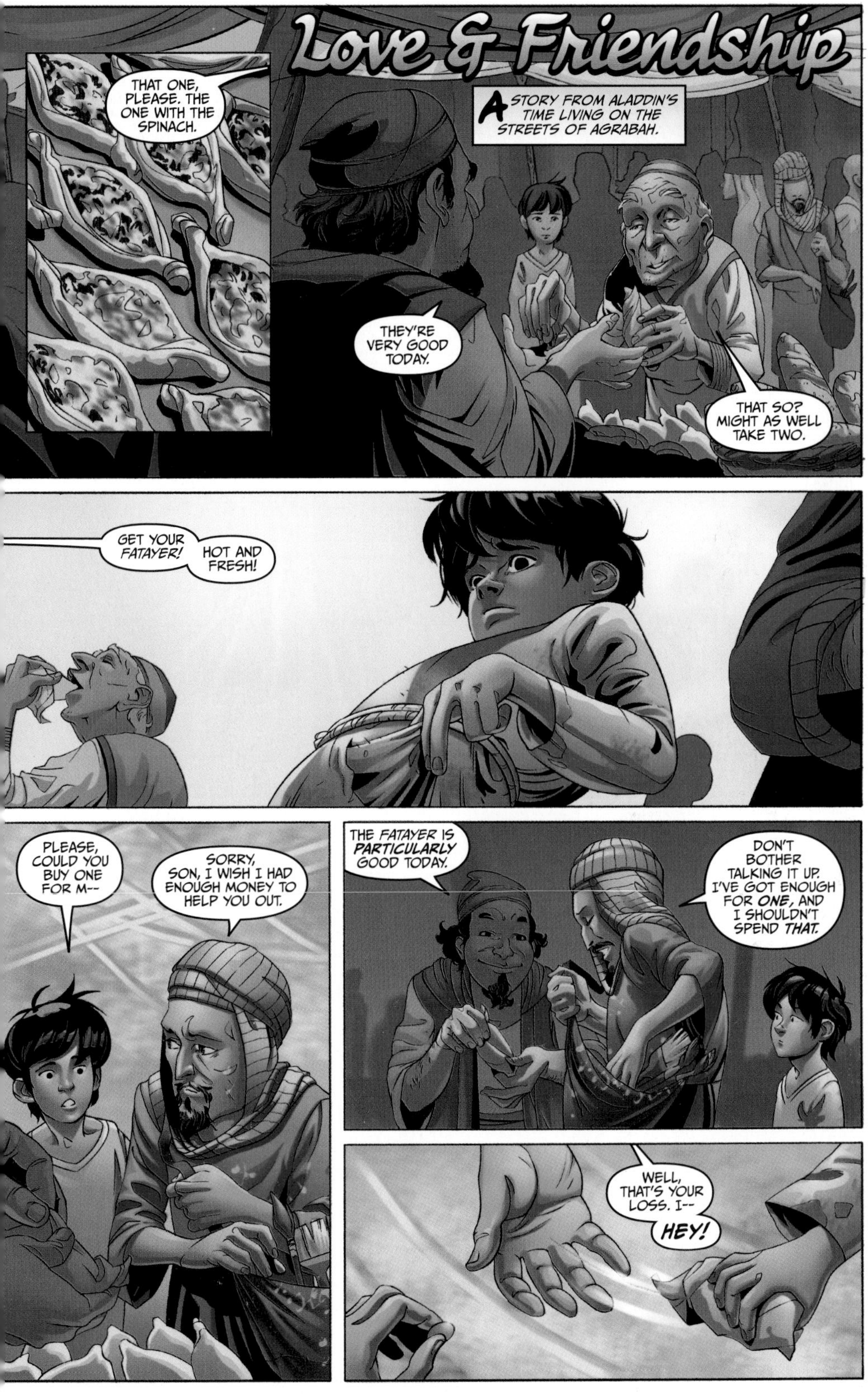

Love & Friendship
A STORY FROM ALADDIN'S TIME LIVING ON THE STREETS OF AGRABAH.
THAT ONE, PLEASE. THE ONE WITH THE SPINACH.
THEY'RE VERY GOOD TODAY.
THAT SO? MIGHT AS WELL TAKE TWO.
GET YOUR *FATAYER!*
HOT AND FRESH!
PLEASE, COULD YOU BUY ONE FOR M--
SORRY, SON, I WISH I HAD ENOUGH MONEY TO HELP YOU OUT.
THE *FATAYER* IS ***PARTICULARLY*** GOOD TODAY.
DON'T BOTHER TALKING IT UP. I'VE GOT ENOUGH FOR ***ONE,*** AND I SHOULDN'T SPEND ***THAT.***
WELL, THAT'S YOUR LOSS. I--
HEY!

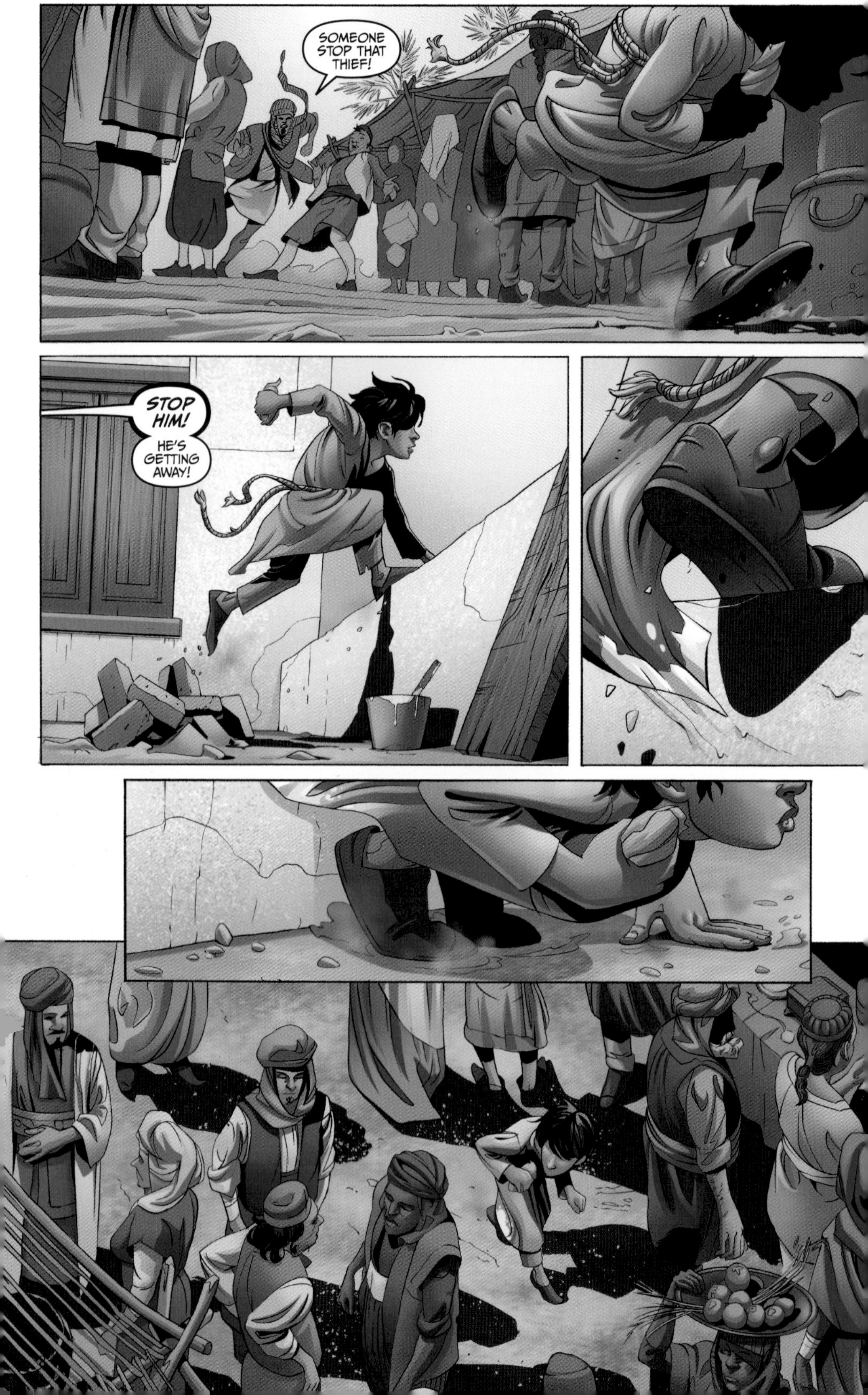
SOMEONE STOP THAT THIEF!
STOP HIM!
HE'S GETTING AWAY!

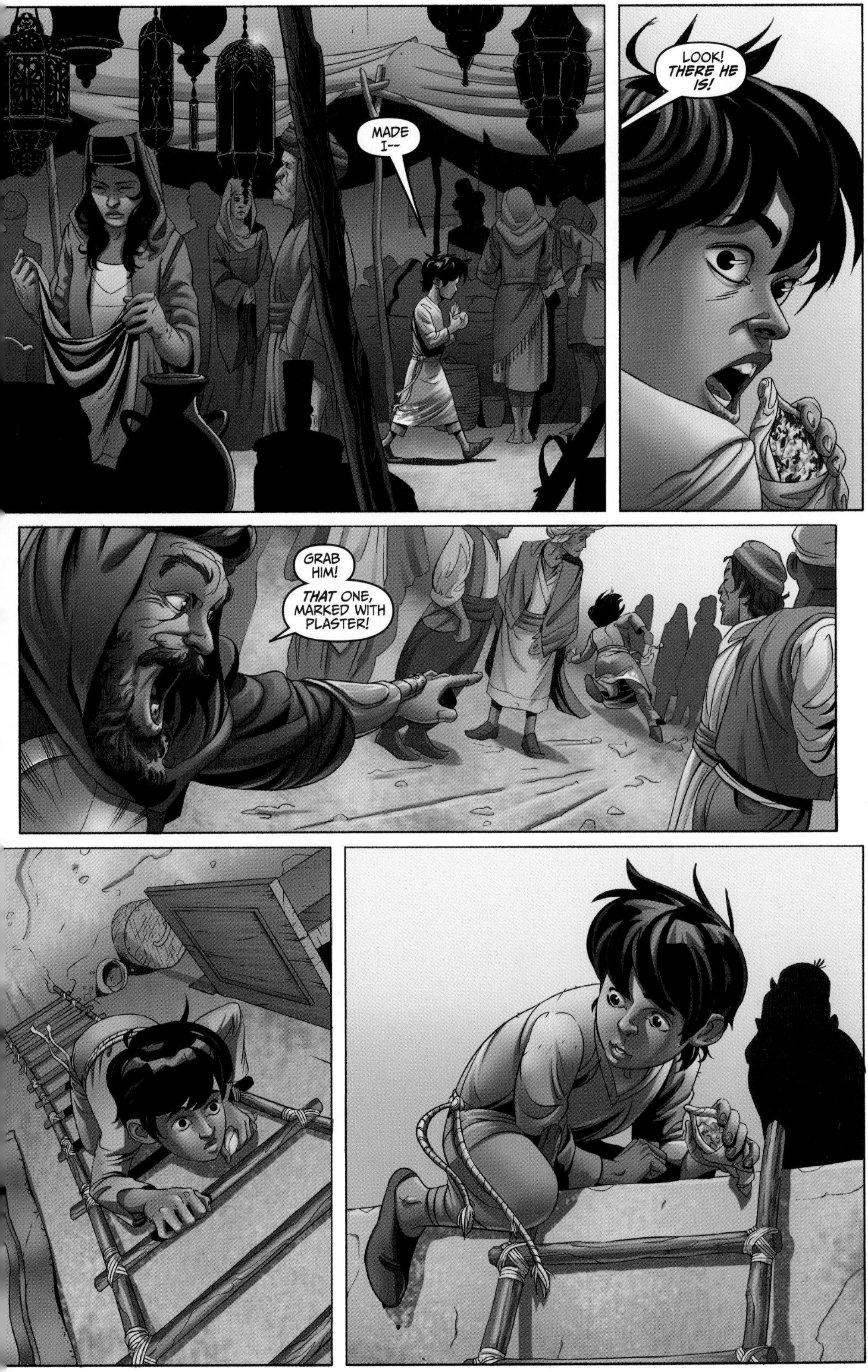
MADE I--
LOOK! THERE HE IS!
GRAB HIM!
THAT ONE, MARKED WITH PLASTER!

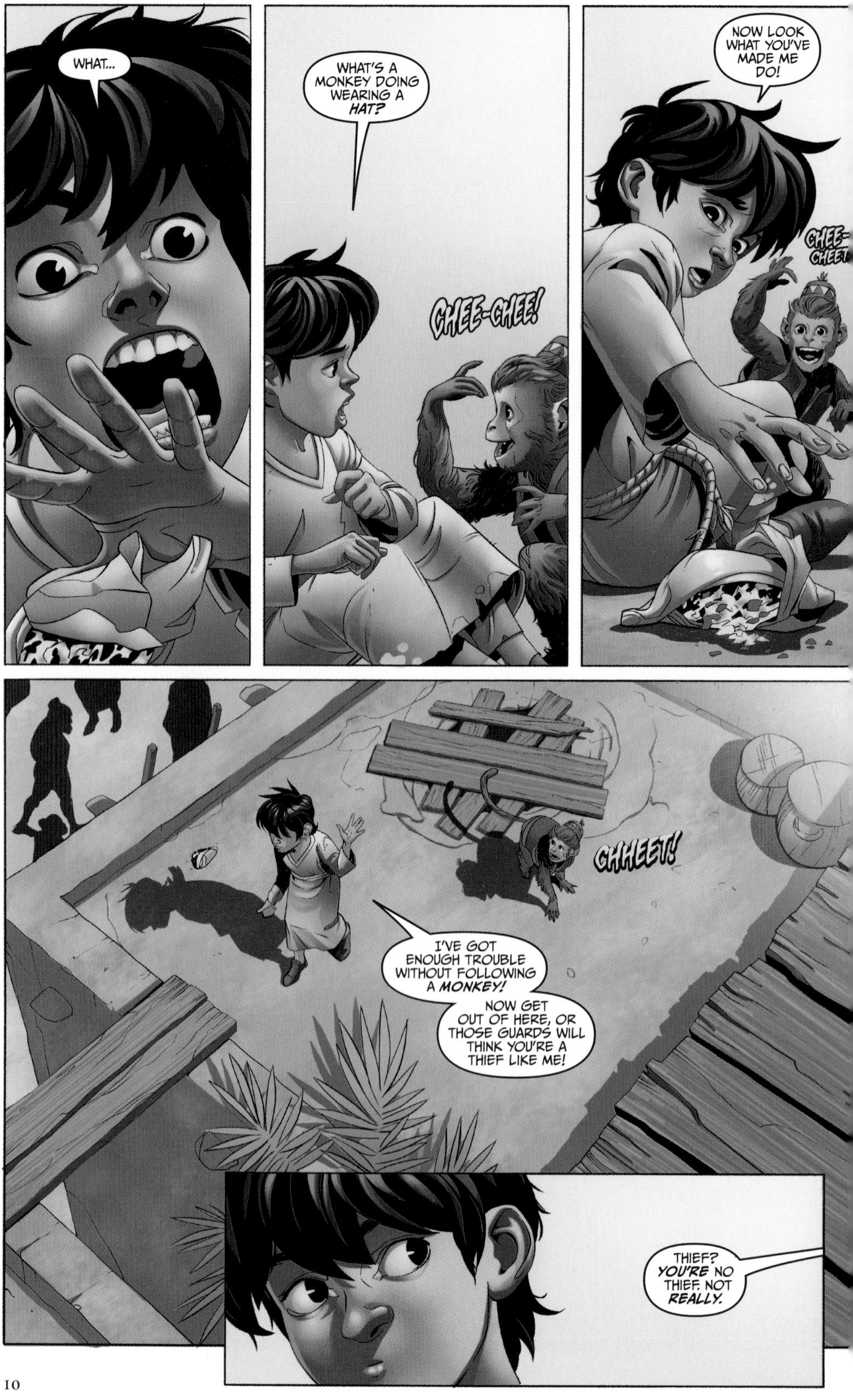
WHAT...
WHAT'S A MONKEY DOING WEARING A HAT?
CHEE-CHEE!
NOW LOOK WHAT YOU'VE MADE ME DO!
CHEE-CHEET!
CHHEET!
I'VE GOT ENOUGH TROUBLE WITHOUT FOLLOWING A MONKEY!
NOW GET OUT OF HERE, OR THOSE GUARDS WILL THINK YOU'RE A THIEF LIKE ME!
THIEF? YOU'RE NO THIEF. NOT REALLY.

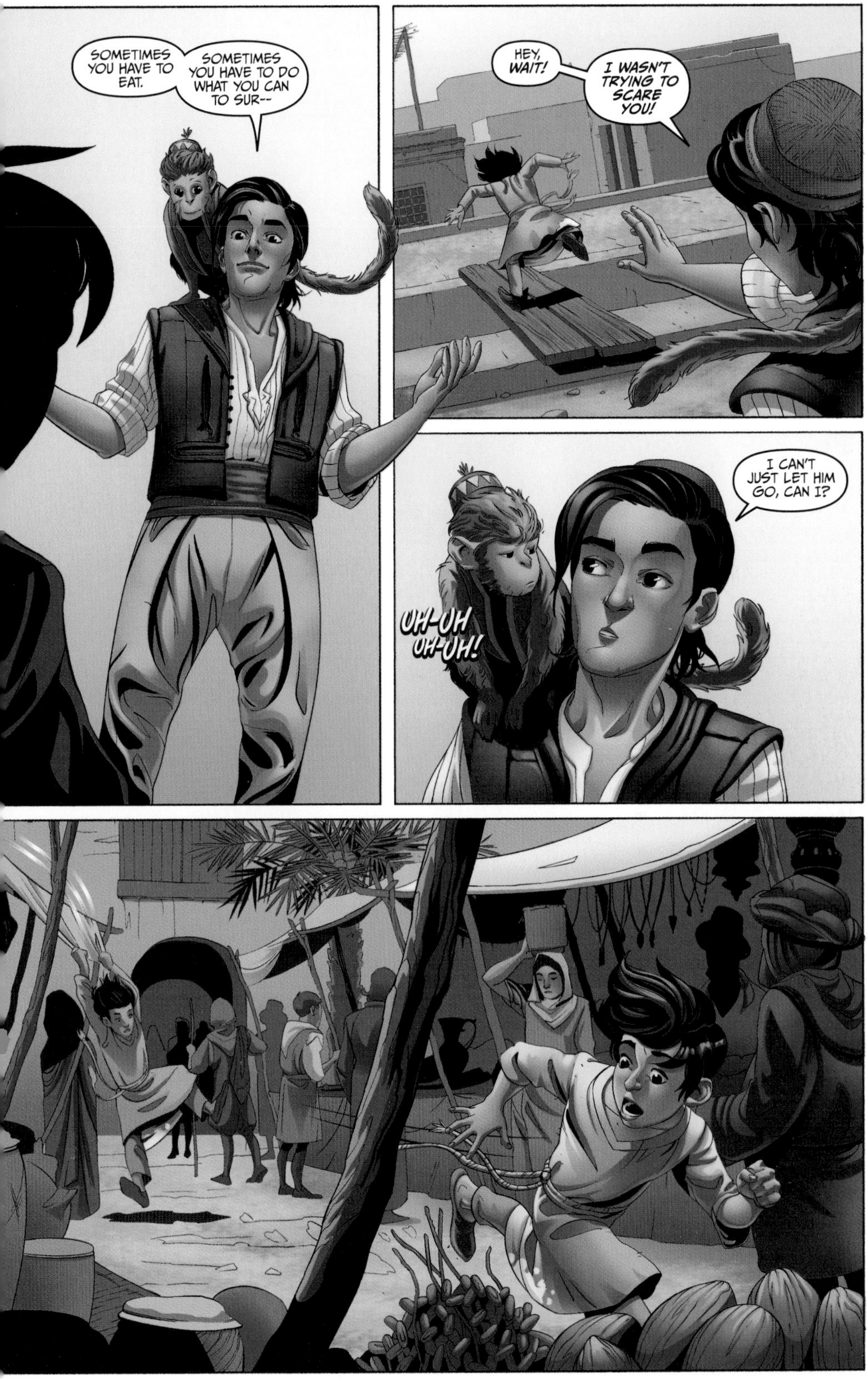
SOMETIMES YOU HAVE TO EAT.
SOMETIMES YOU HAVE TO DO WHAT YOU CAN TO SUR--
HEY, WAIT!
I WASN'T TRYING TO SCARE YOU!
I CAN'T JUST LET HIM GO, CAN I?
UH-UH UH-UH!

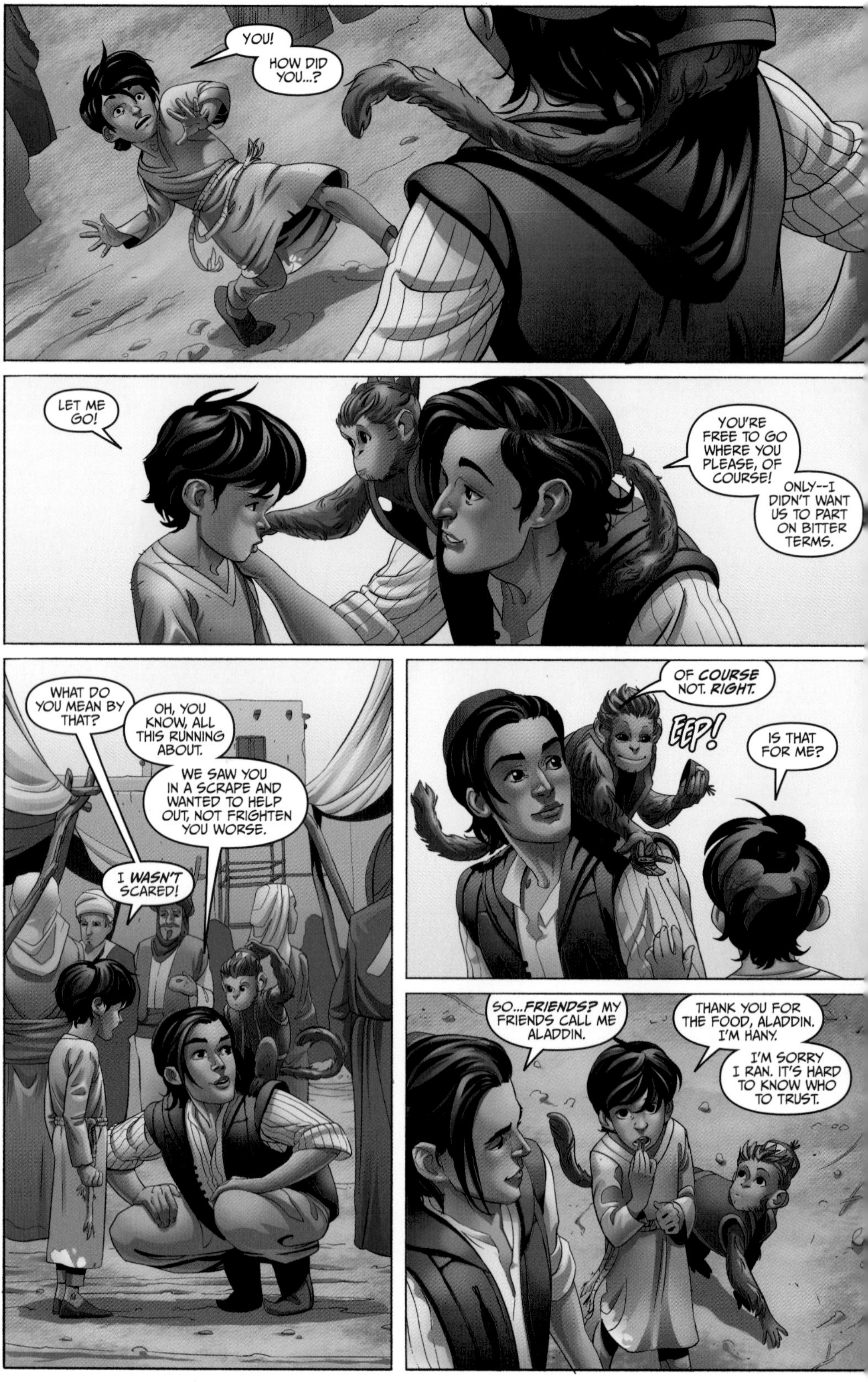
YOU!
HOW DID YOU...?
LET ME GO!
YOU'RE FREE TO GO WHERE YOU PLEASE, OF COURSE!
ONLY--I DIDN'T WANT US TO PART ON BITTER TERMS.
WHAT DO YOU MEAN BY THAT?
OH, YOU KNOW, ALL THIS RUNNING ABOUT.
WE SAW YOU IN A SCRAPE AND WANTED TO HELP OUT, NOT FRIGHTEN YOU WORSE.
I WASN'T SCARED!
OF COURSE NOT. RIGHT.
EEP!
IS THAT FOR ME?
SO...FRIENDS? MY FRIENDS CALL ME ALADDIN.
THANK YOU FOR THE FOOD, ALADDIN. I'M HANY.
I'M SORRY I RAN. IT'S HARD TO KNOW WHO TO TRUST.

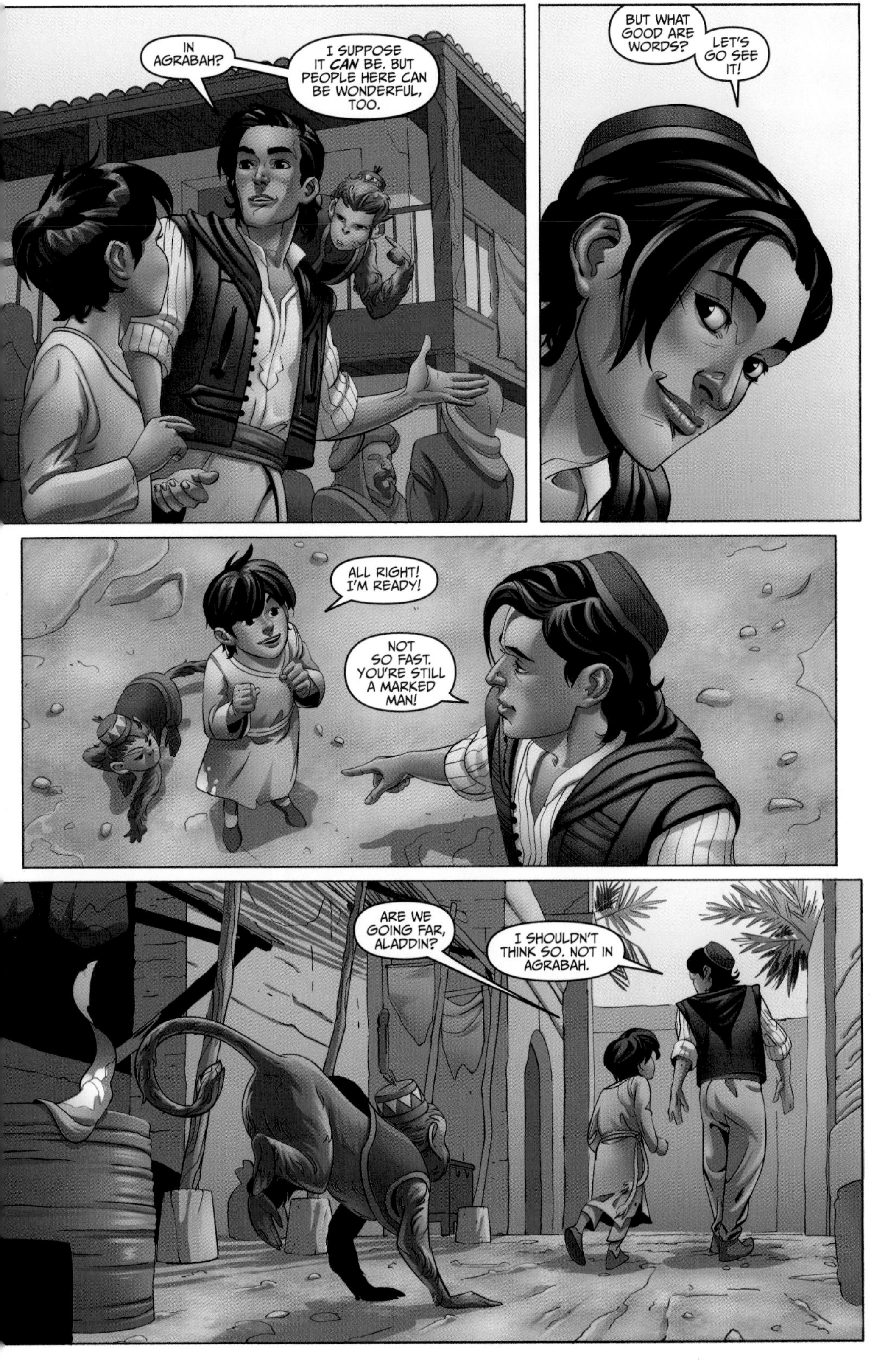
IN AGRABAH?
I SUPPOSE IT CAN BE. BUT PEOPLE HERE CAN BE WONDERFUL, TOO.
BUT WHAT GOOD ARE WORDS?
LET'S GO SEE IT!
ALL RIGHT! I'M READY!
NOT SO FAST. YOU'RE STILL A MARKED MAN!
ARE WE GOING FAR, ALADDIN?
I SHOULDN'T THINK SO. NOT IN AGRABAH.

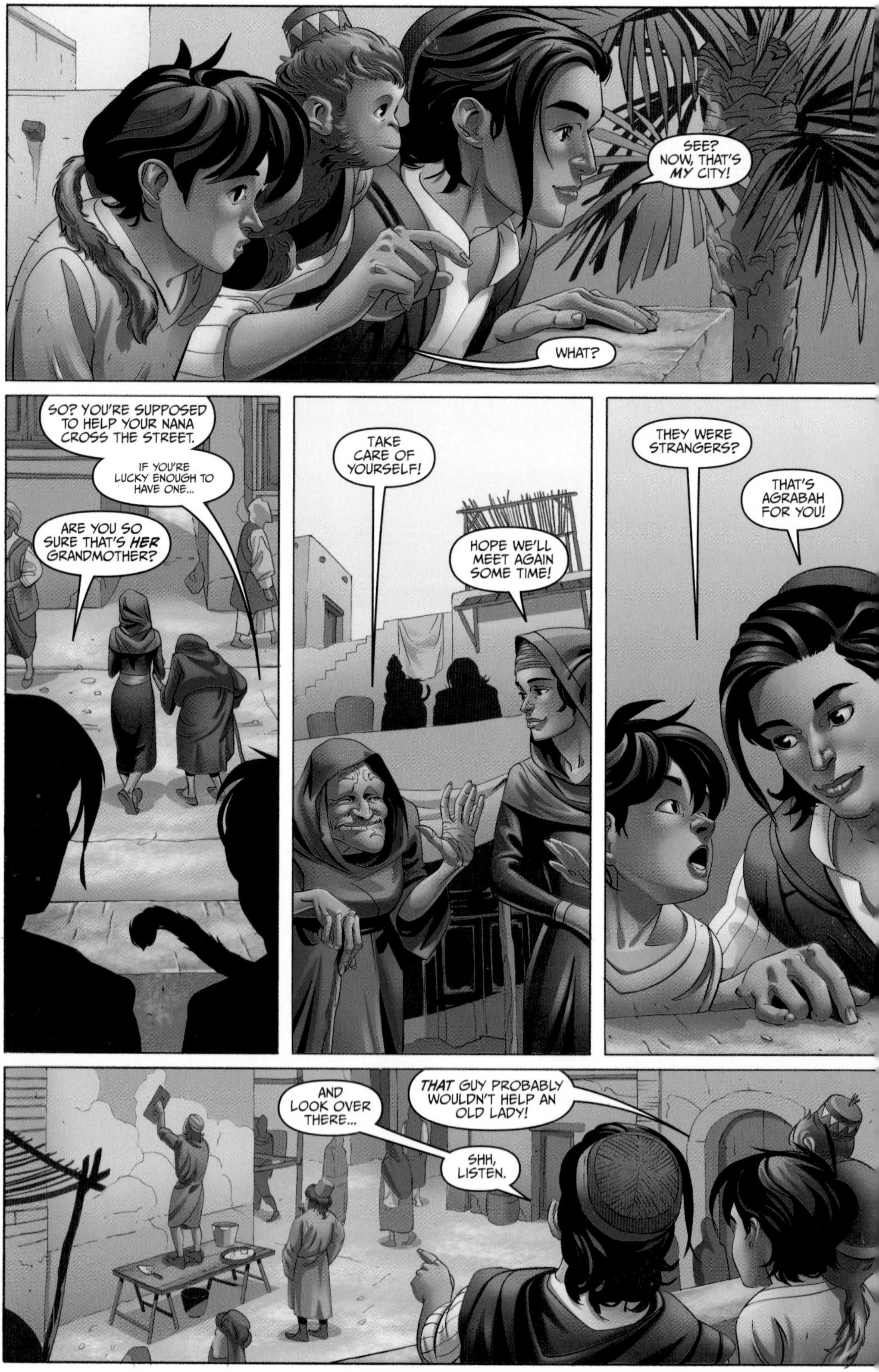
SEE? NOW, THAT'S MY CITY!
WHAT?
SO? YOU'RE SUPPOSED TO HELP YOUR NANA CROSS THE STREET.
IF YOU'RE LUCKY ENOUGH TO HAVE ONE...
ARE YOU SO SURE THAT'S HER GRANDMOTHER?
TAKE CARE OF YOURSELF!
HOPE WE'LL MEET AGAIN SOME TIME!
THEY WERE STRANGERS?
THAT'S AGRABAH FOR YOU!
AND LOOK OVER THERE...
THAT GUY PROBABLY WOULDN'T HELP AN OLD LADY!
SHH, LISTEN.

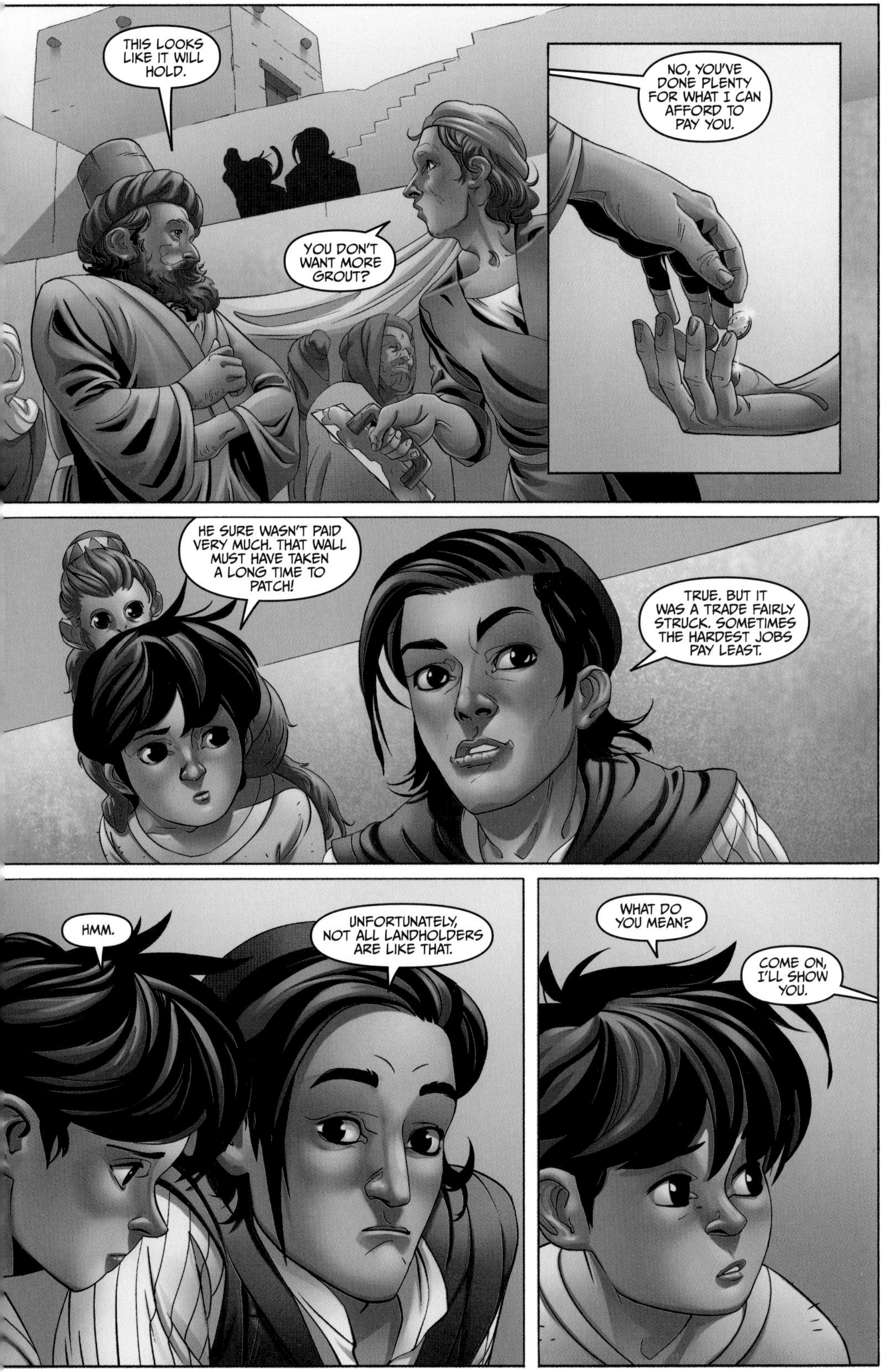

THIS LOOKS LIKE IT WILL HOLD.
YOU DON'T WANT MORE GROUT?
NO, YOU'VE DONE PLENTY FOR WHAT I CAN AFFORD TO PAY YOU.
HE SURE WASN'T PAID VERY MUCH. THAT WALL MUST HAVE TAKEN A LONG TIME TO PATCH!
TRUE. BUT IT WAS A TRADE FAIRLY STRUCK. SOMETIMES THE HARDEST JOBS PAY LEAST.
HMM.
UNFORTUNATELY, NOT ALL LANDHOLDERS ARE LIKE THAT.
WHAT DO YOU MEAN?
COME ON, I'LL SHOW YOU.

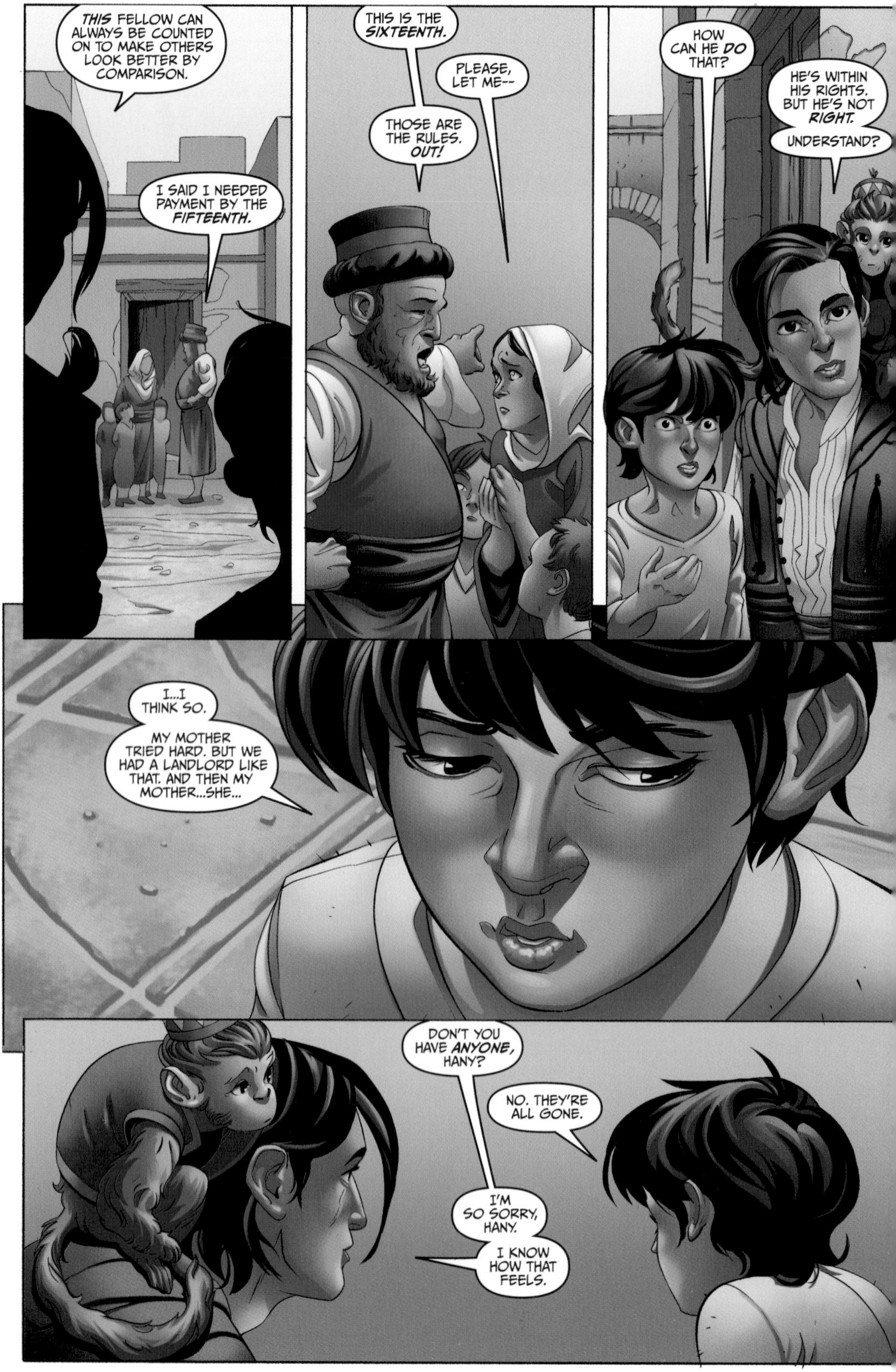
THIS FELLOW CAN ALWAYS BE COUNTED ON TO MAKE OTHERS LOOK BETTER BY COMPARISON.
I SAID I NEEDED PAYMENT BY THE FIFTEENTH.
THIS IS THE SIXTEENTH.
PLEASE, LET ME--
THOSE ARE THE RULES. OUT!
HOW CAN HE DO THAT?
HE'S WITHIN HIS RIGHTS. BUT HE'S NOT RIGHT.
UNDERSTAND?
I...I THINK SO.
MY MOTHER TRIED HARD. BUT WE HAD A LANDLORD LIKE THAT. AND THEN MY MOTHER...SHE...
DON'T YOU HAVE ANYONE, HANY?
NO. THEY'RE ALL GONE.
I'M SO SORRY, HANY.
I KNOW HOW THAT FEELS.

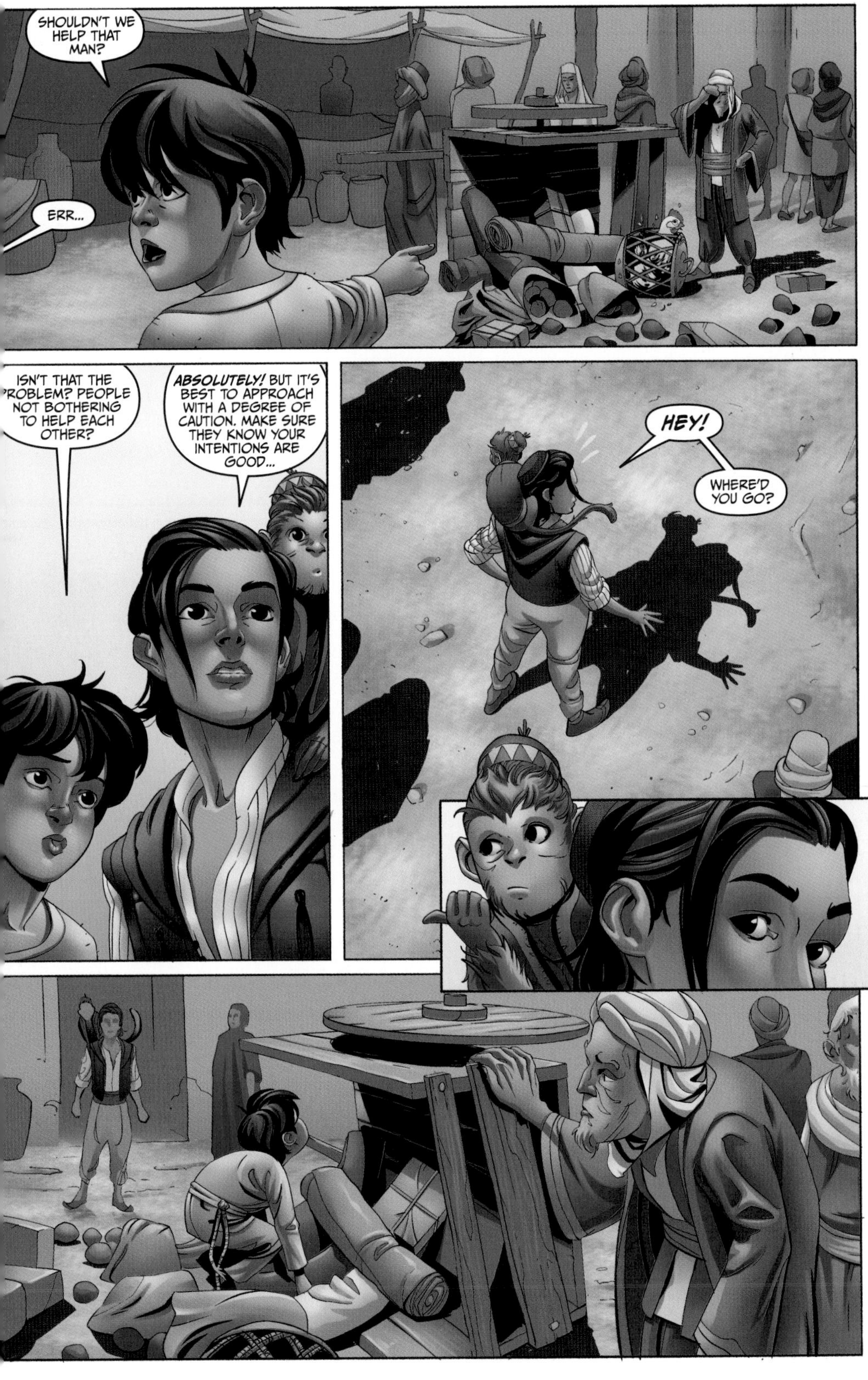
SHOULDN'T WE HELP THAT MAN?
ERR...
ISN'T THAT THE PROBLEM? PEOPLE NOT BOTHERING TO HELP EACH OTHER?
ABSOLUTELY! BUT IT'S BEST TO APPROACH WITH A DEGREE OF CAUTION. MAKE SURE THEY KNOW YOUR INTENTIONS ARE GOOD...
HEY!
WHERE'D YOU GO?

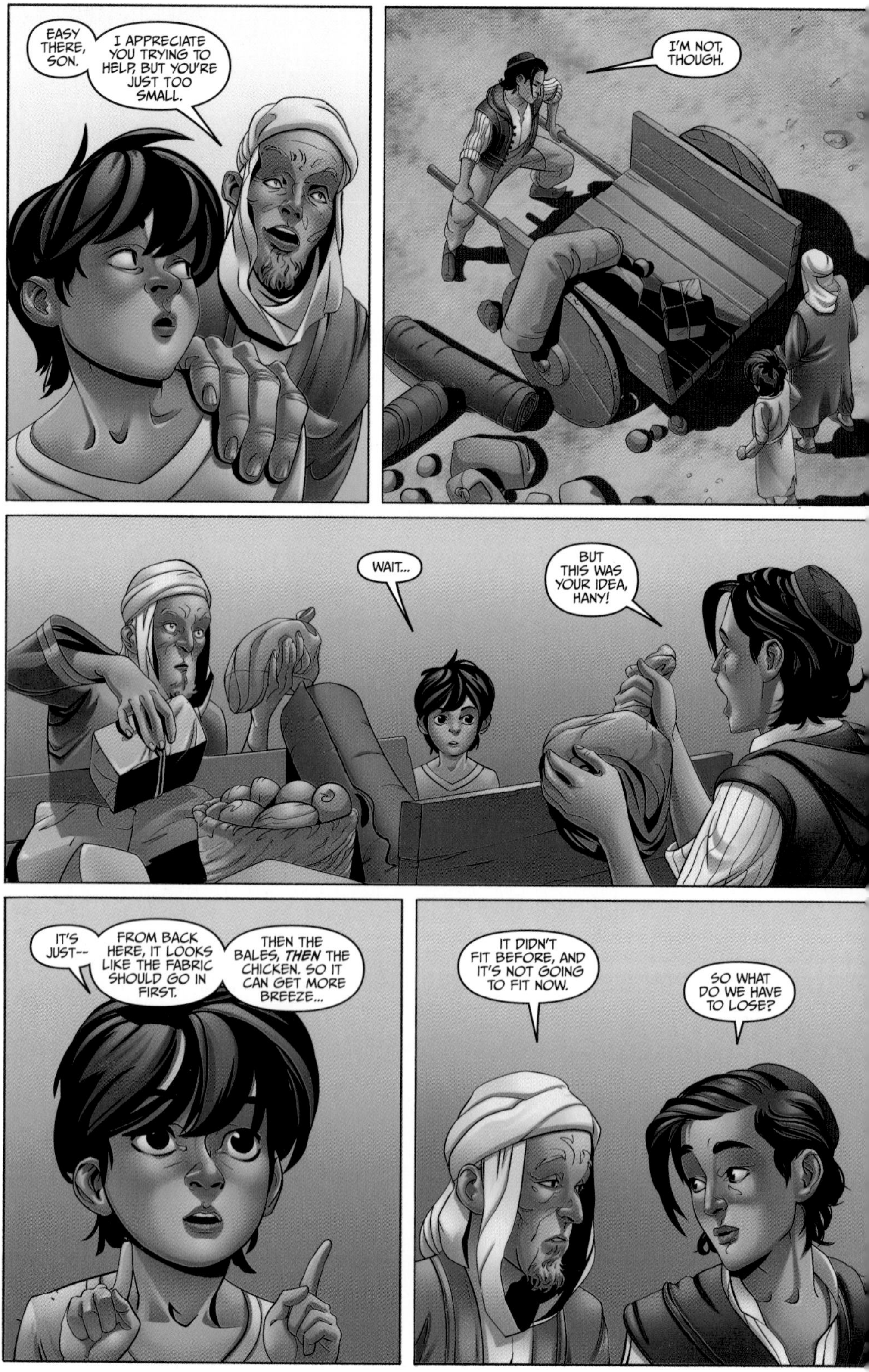
EASY THERE, SON.
I APPRECIATE YOU TRYING TO HELP, BUT YOU'RE JUST TOO SMALL.
I'M NOT, THOUGH.
WAIT...
BUT THIS WAS YOUR IDEA, HANY!
IT'S JUST--
FROM BACK HERE, IT LOOKS LIKE THE FABRIC SHOULD GO IN FIRST.
THEN THE BALES, *THEN* THE CHICKEN. SO IT CAN GET MORE BREEZE...
IT DIDN'T FIT BEFORE, AND IT'S NOT GOING TO FIT NOW.
SO WHAT DO WE HAVE TO LOSE?

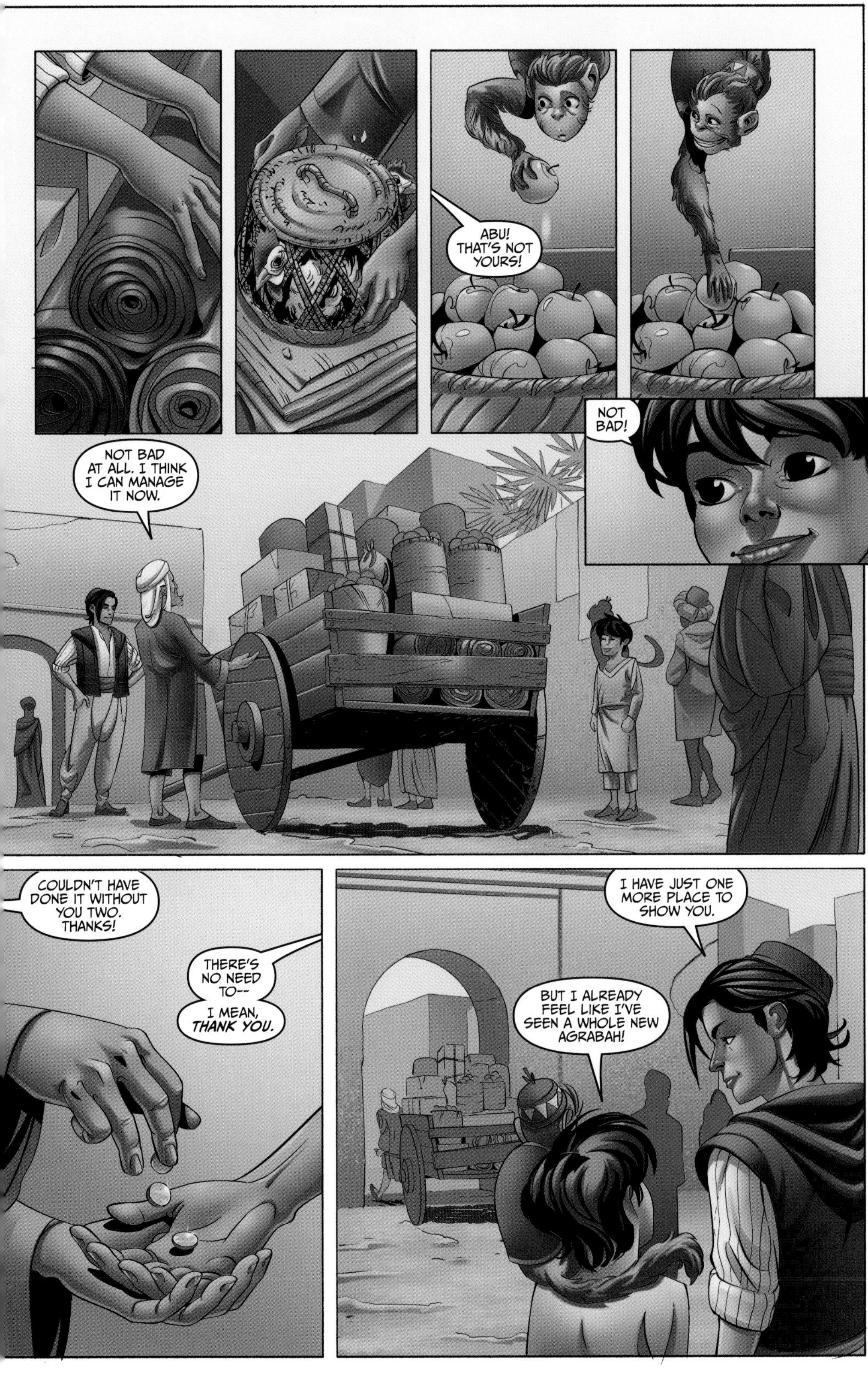
ABU! THAT'S NOT YOURS!
NOT BAD!
NOT BAD AT ALL. I THINK I CAN MANAGE IT NOW.
COULDN'T HAVE DONE IT WITHOUT YOU TWO. THANKS!
THERE'S NO NEED TO--
I MEAN, THANK YOU.
I HAVE JUST ONE MORE PLACE TO SHOW YOU.
BUT I ALREADY FEEL LIKE I'VE SEEN A WHOLE NEW AGRABAH!

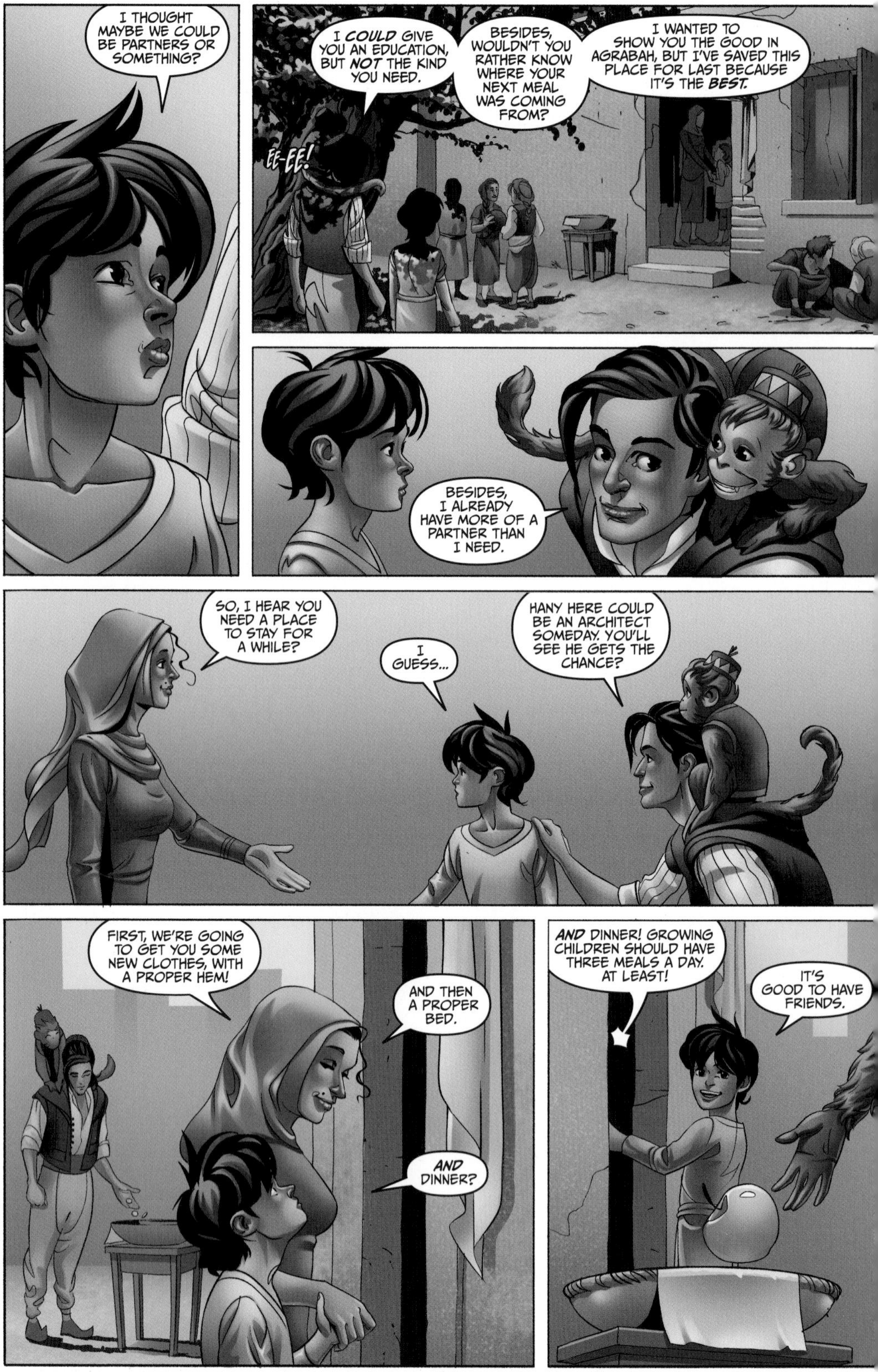
I THOUGHT MAYBE WE COULD BE PARTNERS OR SOMETHING?
I COULD GIVE YOU AN EDUCATION, BUT NOT THE KIND YOU NEED.
BESIDES, WOULDN'T YOU RATHER KNOW WHERE YOUR NEXT MEAL WAS COMING FROM?
I WANTED TO SHOW YOU THE GOOD IN AGRABAH, BUT I'VE SAVED THIS PLACE FOR LAST BECAUSE IT'S THE BEST.
EE-EE!
BESIDES, I ALREADY HAVE MORE OF A PARTNER THAN I NEED.
SO, I HEAR YOU NEED A PLACE TO STAY FOR A WHILE?
I GUESS...
HANY HERE COULD BE AN ARCHITECT SOMEDAY. YOU'LL SEE HE GETS THE CHANCE?
FIRST, WE'RE GOING TO GET YOU SOME NEW CLOTHES, WITH A PROPER HEM!
AND THEN A PROPER BED.
AND DINNER?
AND DINNER! GROWING CHILDREN SHOULD HAVE THREE MEALS A DAY. AT LEAST!
IT'S GOOD TO HAVE FRIENDS.

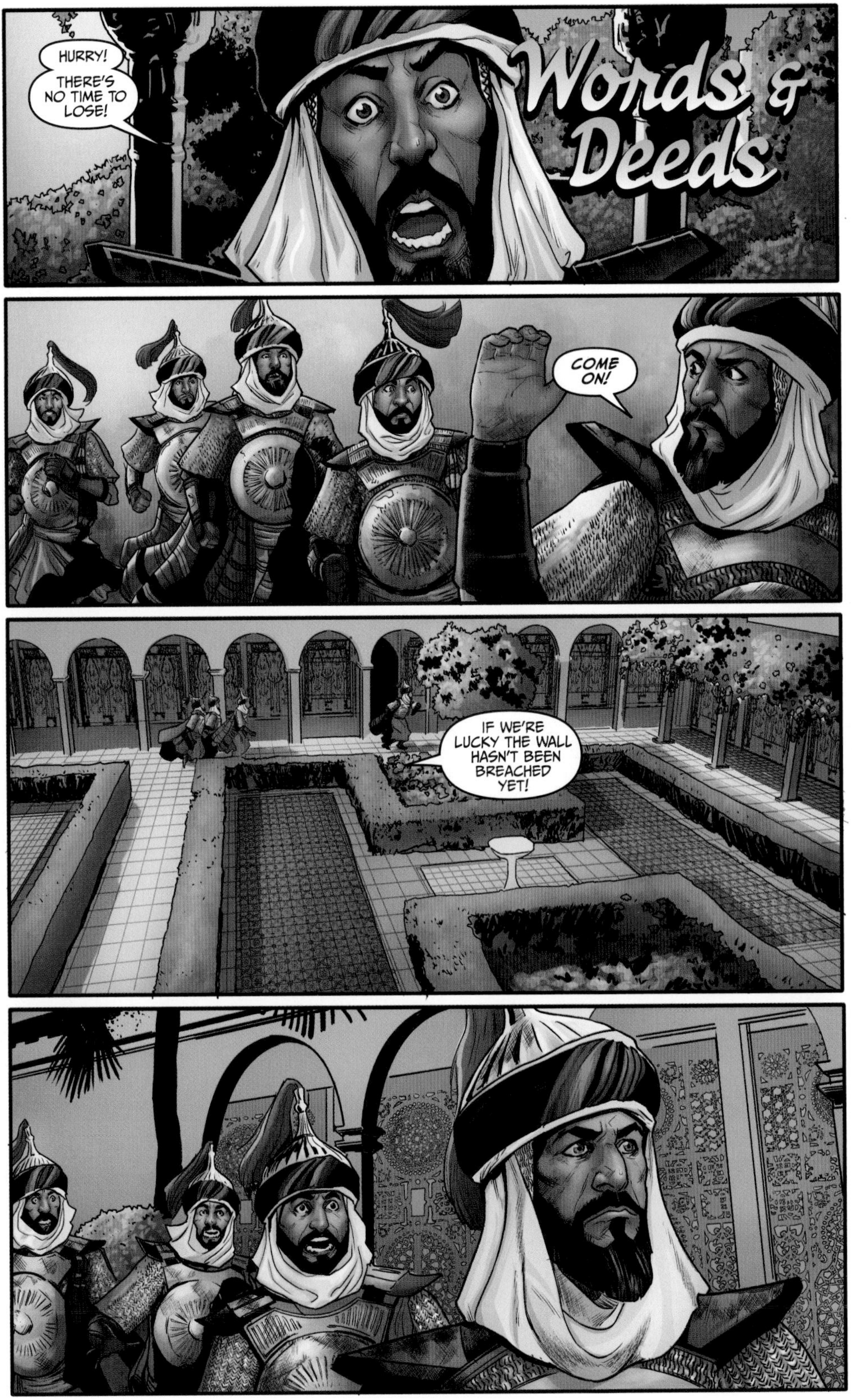
Words & Deeds
HURRY! THERE'S NO TIME TO LOSE!
COME ON!
IF WE'RE LUCKY THE WALL HASN'T BEEN BREACHED YET!

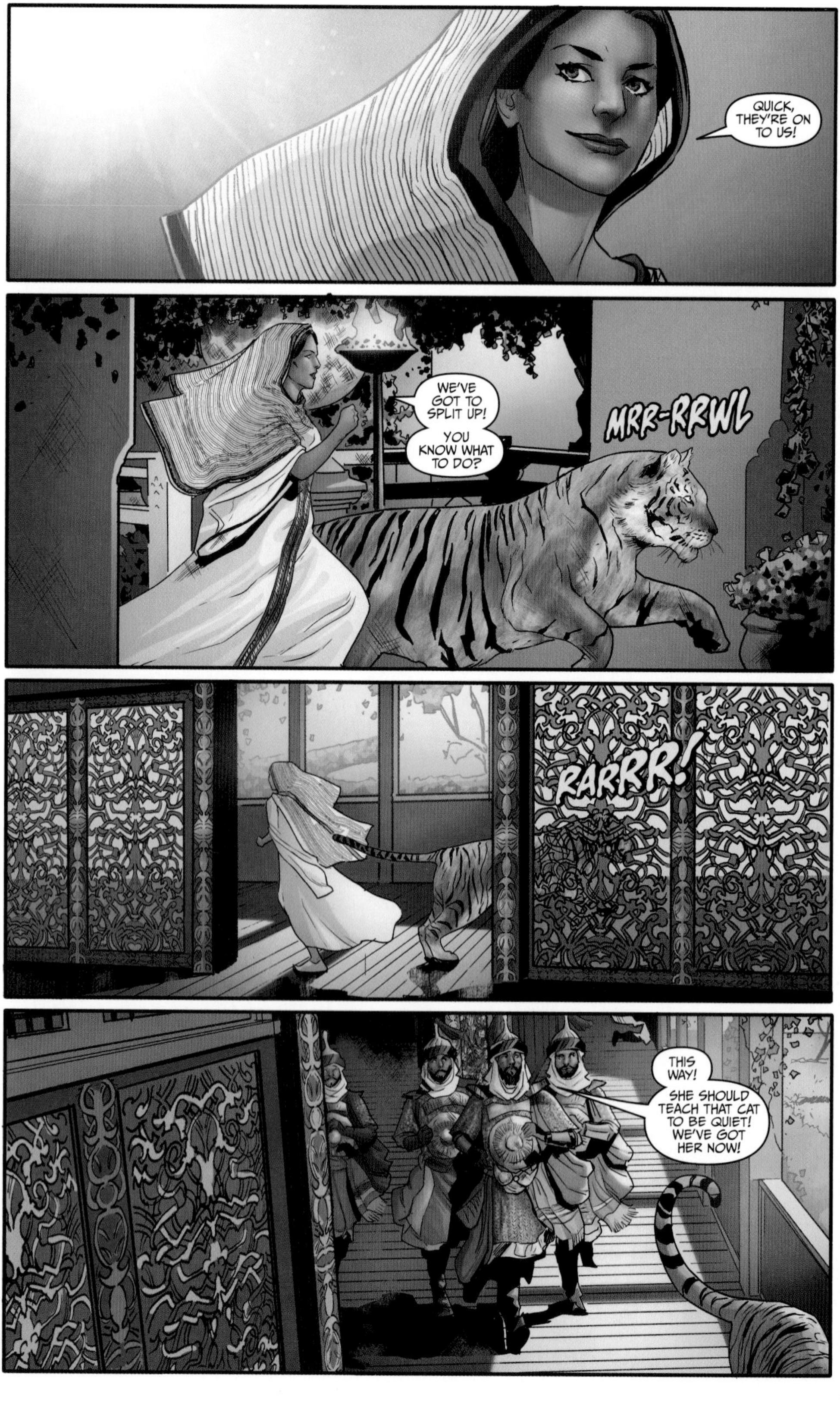
QUICK, THEY'RE ON TO US!
WE'VE GOT TO SPLIT UP!
YOU KNOW WHAT TO DO?
MRR-RRWL
RARRR!
THIS WAY!
SHE SHOULD TEACH THAT CAT TO BE QUIET! WE'VE GOT HER NOW!

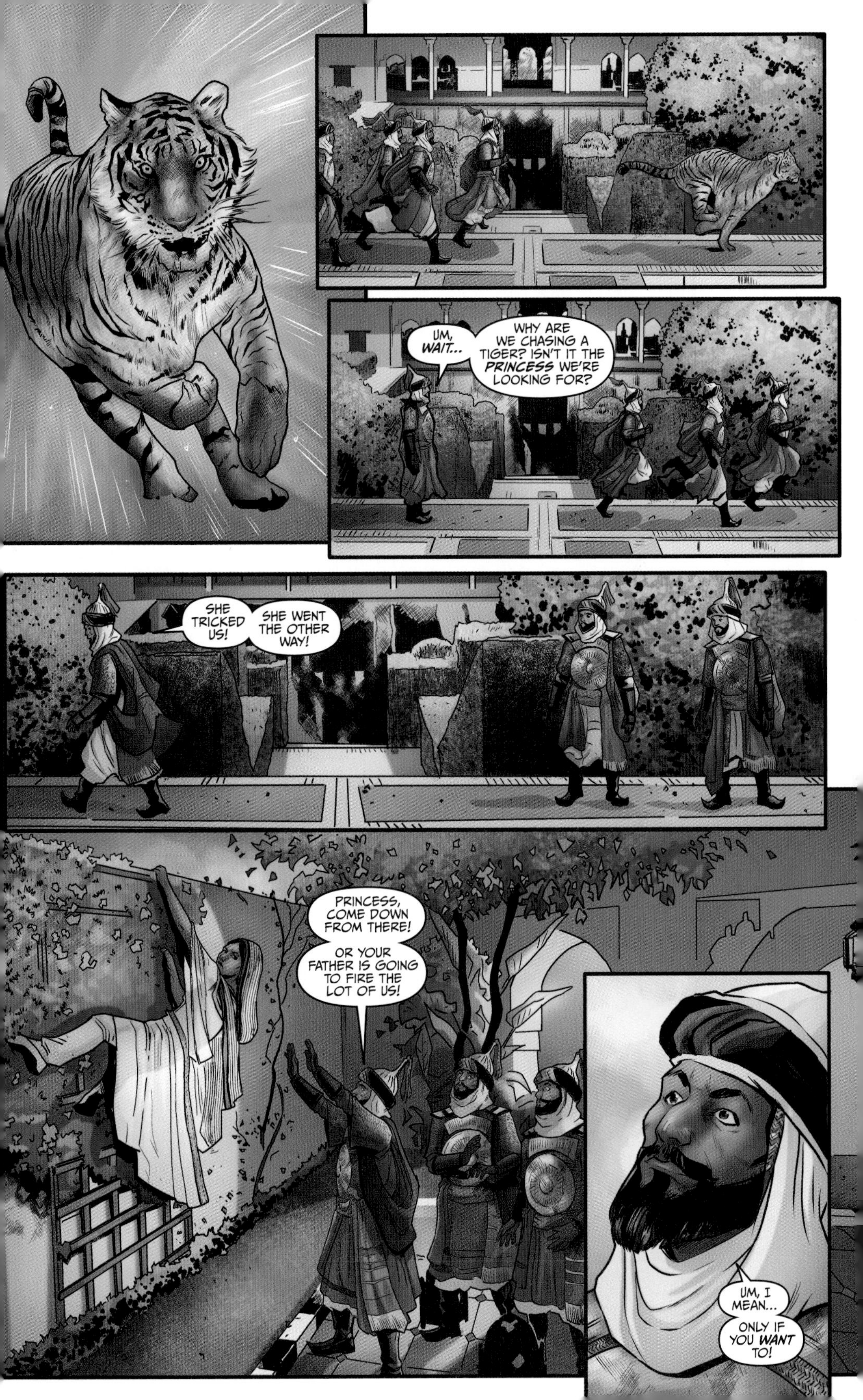
UM, WAIT...
WHY ARE WE CHASING A TIGER? ISN'T IT THE PRINCESS WE'RE LOOKING FOR?
SHE TRICKED US!
SHE WENT THE OTHER WAY!
PRINCESS, COME DOWN FROM THERE!
OR YOUR FATHER IS GOING TO FIRE THE LOT OF US!
UM, I MEAN...
ONLY IF YOU WANT TO!

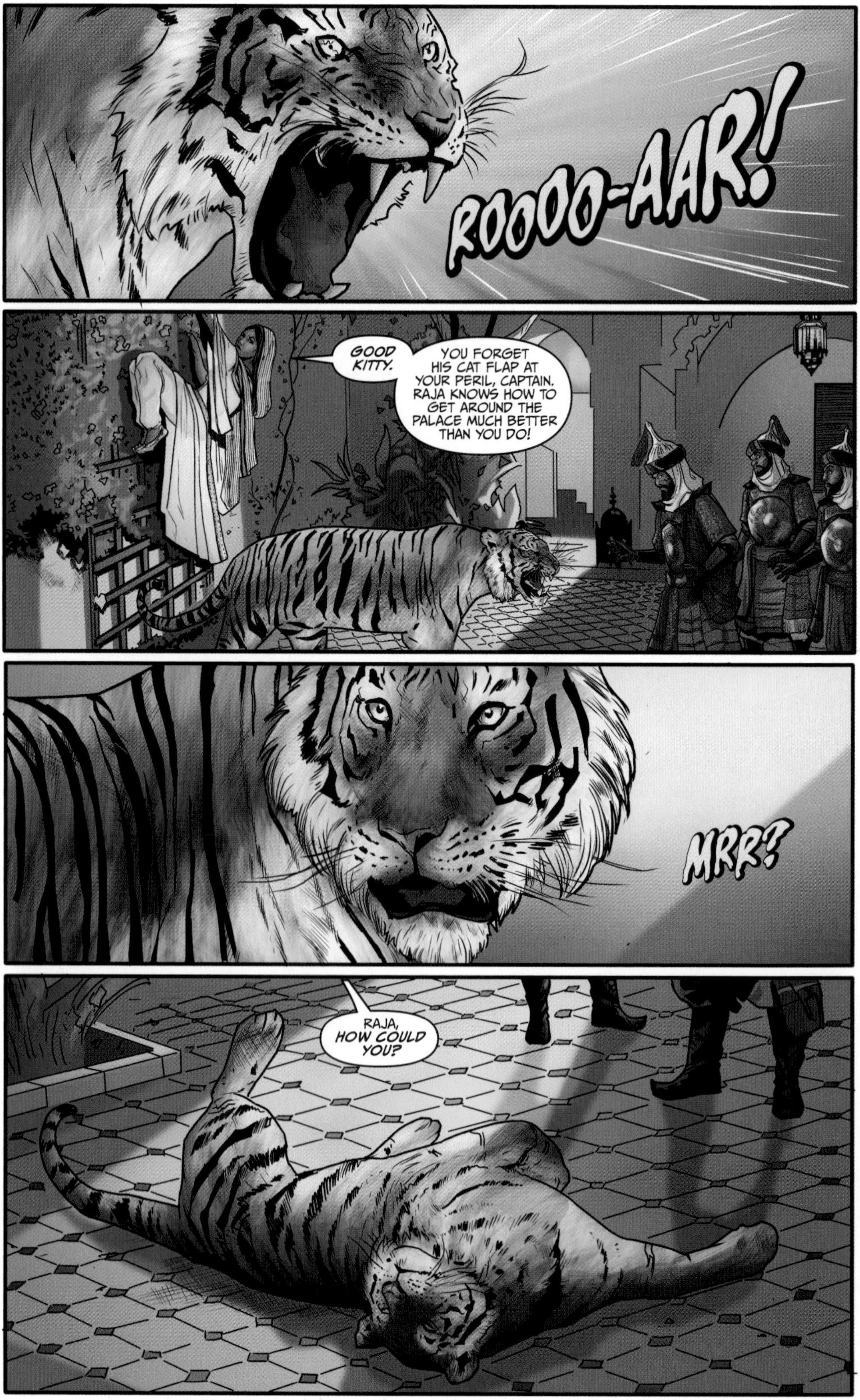
ROOOO-AAR!
GOOD KITTY.
YOU FORGET HIS CAT FLAP AT YOUR PERIL, CAPTAIN. RAJA KNOWS HOW TO GET AROUND THE PALACE MUCH BETTER THAN YOU DO!
MRR?
RAJA, HOW COULD YOU?

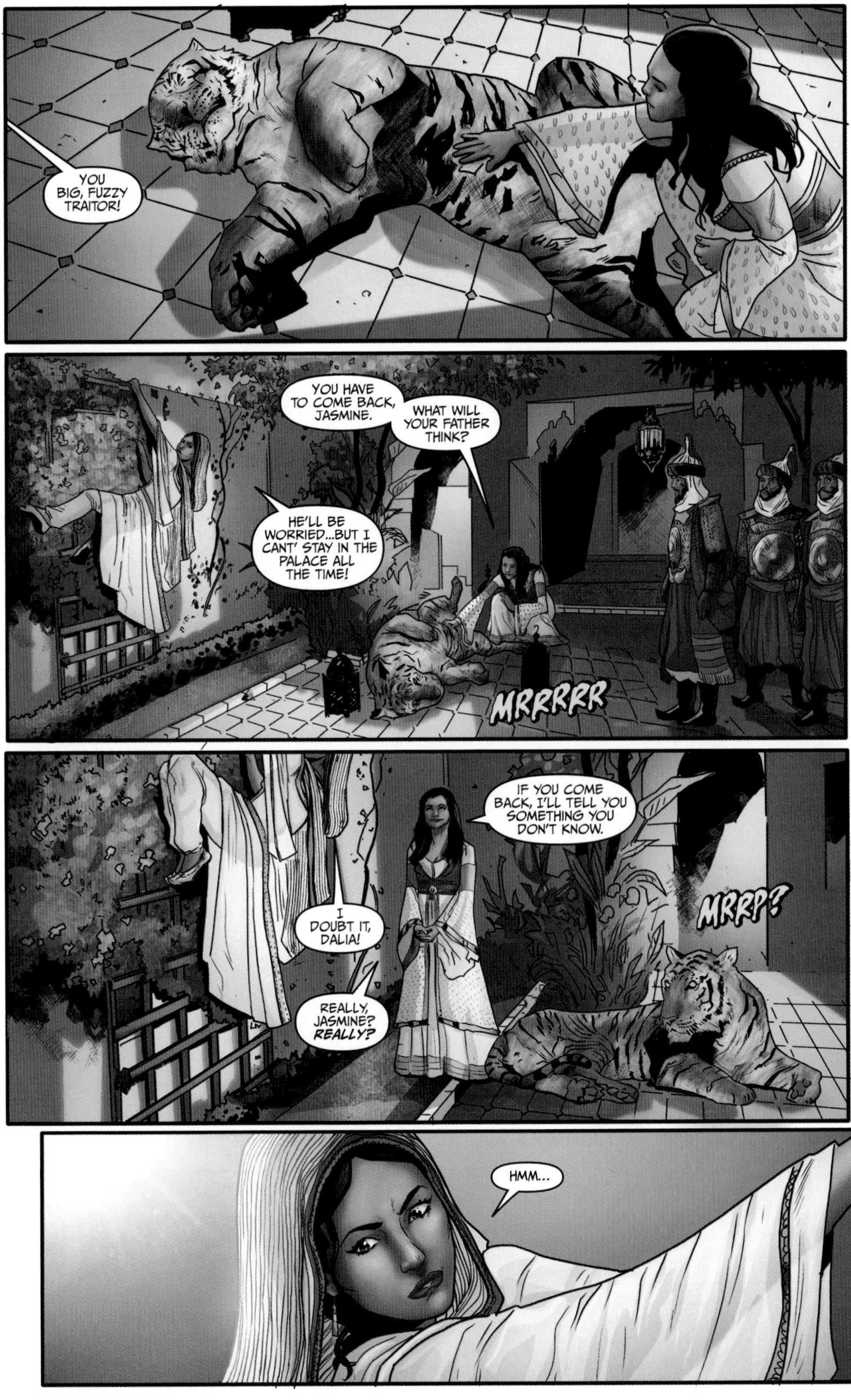
YOU BIG, FUZZY TRAITOR!
YOU HAVE TO COME BACK, JASMINE.
WHAT WILL YOUR FATHER THINK?
HE'LL BE WORRIED...BUT I CANT' STAY IN THE PALACE ALL THE TIME!
MRRRRR
IF YOU COME BACK, I'LL TELL YOU SOMETHING YOU DON'T KNOW.
I DOUBT IT, DALIA!
REALLY, JASMINE? *REALLY?*
MRRP?
HMM...

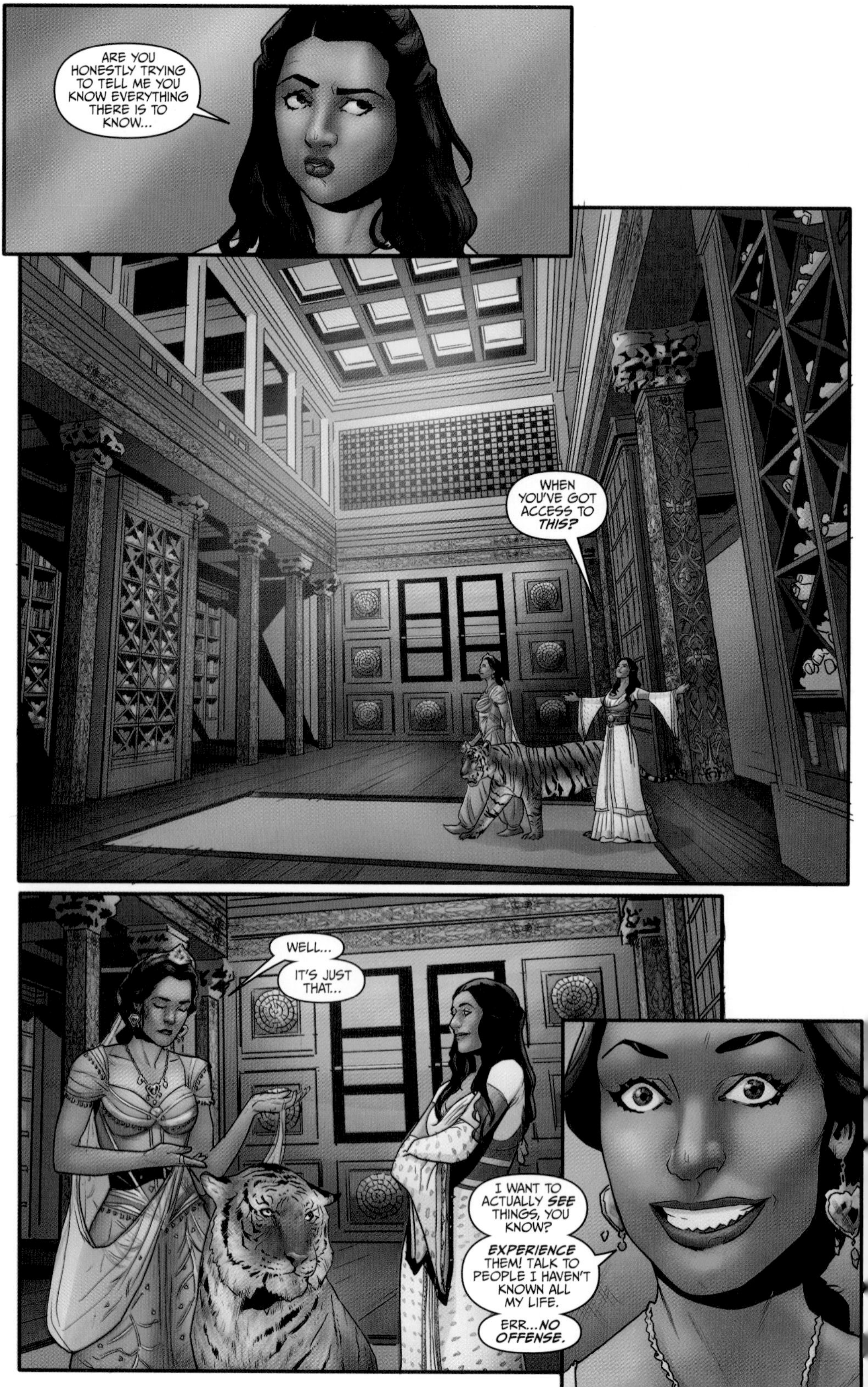
ARE YOU HONESTLY TRYING TO TELL ME YOU KNOW EVERYTHING THERE IS TO KNOW...
WHEN YOU'VE GOT ACCESS TO *THIS?*
WELL...
IT'S JUST THAT...
I WANT TO ACTUALLY *SEE* THINGS, YOU KNOW?
EXPERIENCE THEM! TALK TO PEOPLE I HAVEN'T KNOWN ALL MY LIFE.
ERR...*NO OFFENSE.*

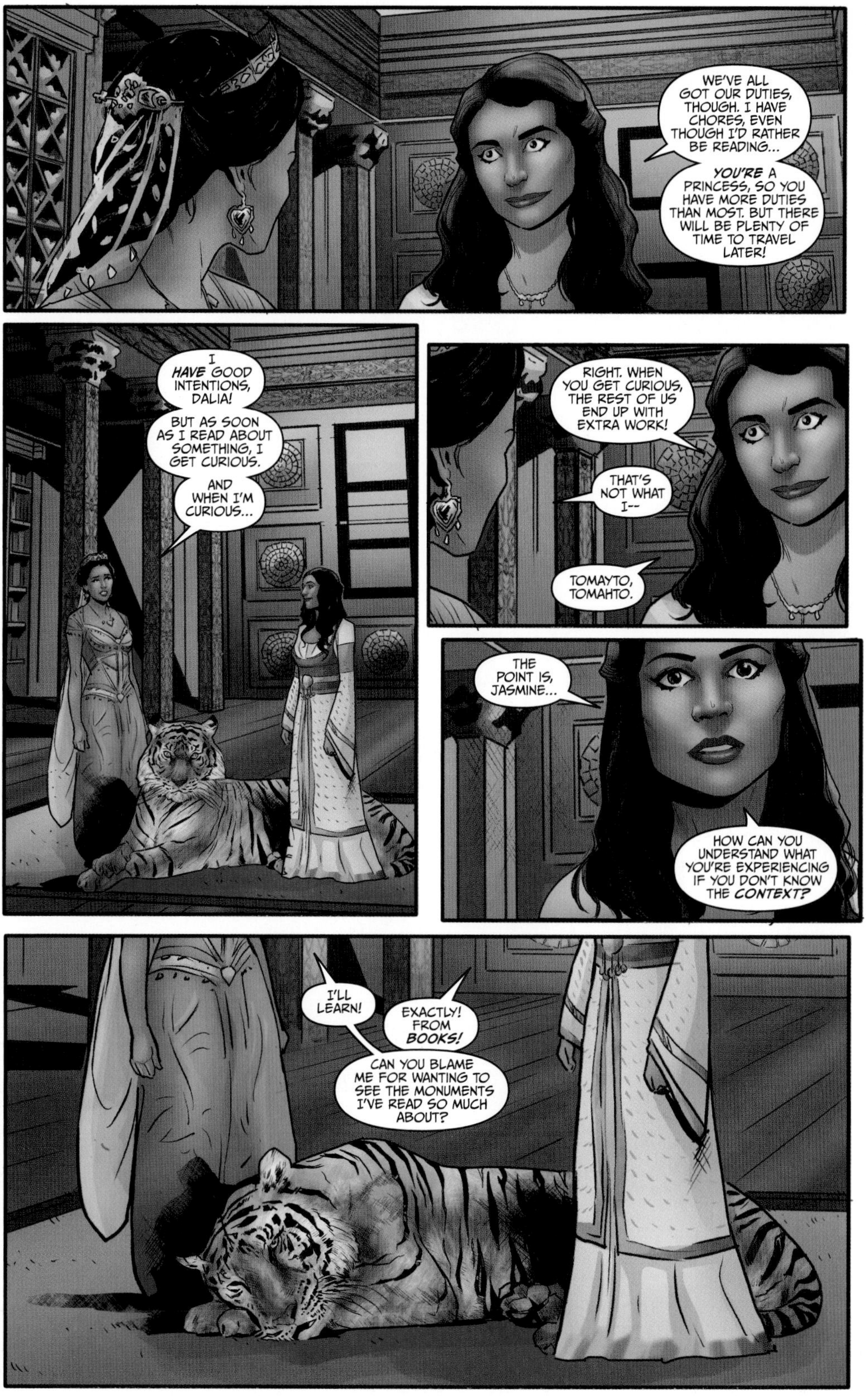
WE'VE ALL GOT OUR DUTIES, THOUGH. I HAVE CHORES, EVEN THOUGH I'D RATHER BE READING...
YOU'RE A PRINCESS, SO YOU HAVE MORE DUTIES THAN MOST. BUT THERE WILL BE PLENTY OF TIME TO TRAVEL LATER!
I HAVE GOOD INTENTIONS, DALIA!
BUT AS SOON AS I READ ABOUT SOMETHING, I GET CURIOUS.
AND WHEN I'M CURIOUS...
RIGHT. WHEN YOU GET CURIOUS, THE REST OF US END UP WITH EXTRA WORK!
THAT'S NOT WHAT I--
TOMAYTO, TOMAHTO.
THE POINT IS, JASMINE...
HOW CAN YOU UNDERSTAND WHAT YOU'RE EXPERIENCING IF YOU DON'T KNOW THE CONTEXT?
I'LL LEARN!
EXACTLY! FROM BOOKS!
CAN YOU BLAME ME FOR WANTING TO SEE THE MONUMENTS I'VE READ SO MUCH ABOUT?

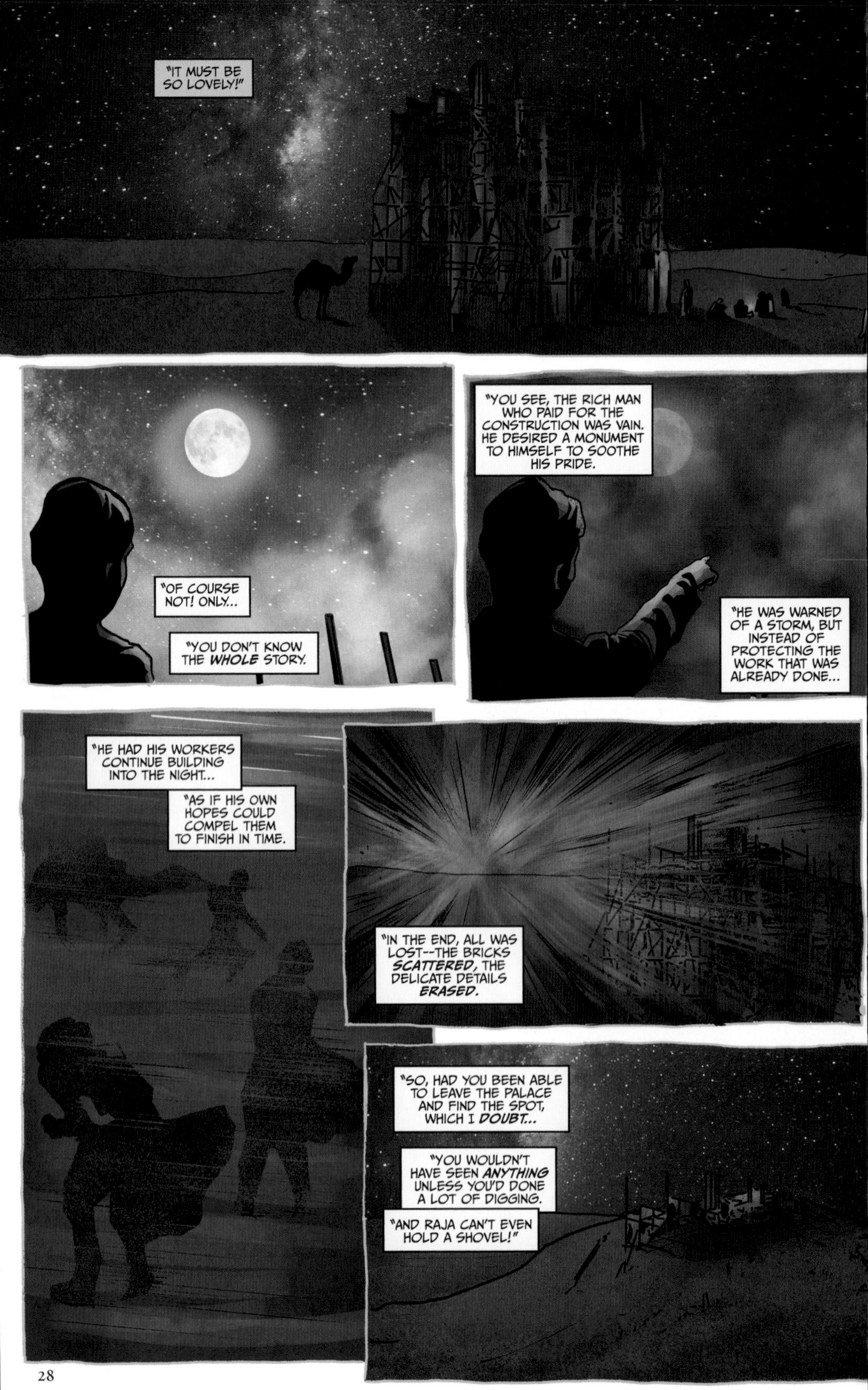
"IT MUST BE SO LOVELY!"
"OF COURSE NOT! ONLY...
"YOU DON'T KNOW THE *WHOLE* STORY.
"YOU SEE, THE RICH MAN WHO PAID FOR THE CONSTRUCTION WAS VAIN. HE DESIRED A MONUMENT TO HIMSELF TO SOOTHE HIS PRIDE.
"HE WAS WARNED OF A STORM, BUT INSTEAD OF PROTECTING THE WORK THAT WAS ALREADY DONE...
"HE HAD HIS WORKERS CONTINUE BUILDING INTO THE NIGHT...
"AS IF HIS OWN HOPES COULD COMPEL THEM TO FINISH IN TIME.
"IN THE END, ALL WAS LOST--THE BRICKS *SCATTERED*, THE DELICATE DETAILS *ERASED*.
"SO, HAD YOU BEEN ABLE TO LEAVE THE PALACE AND FIND THE SPOT, WHICH I *DOUBT*...
"YOU WOULDN'T HAVE SEEN *ANYTHING* UNLESS YOU'D DONE A LOT OF DIGGING.
"AND RAJA CAN'T EVEN HOLD A SHOVEL!"

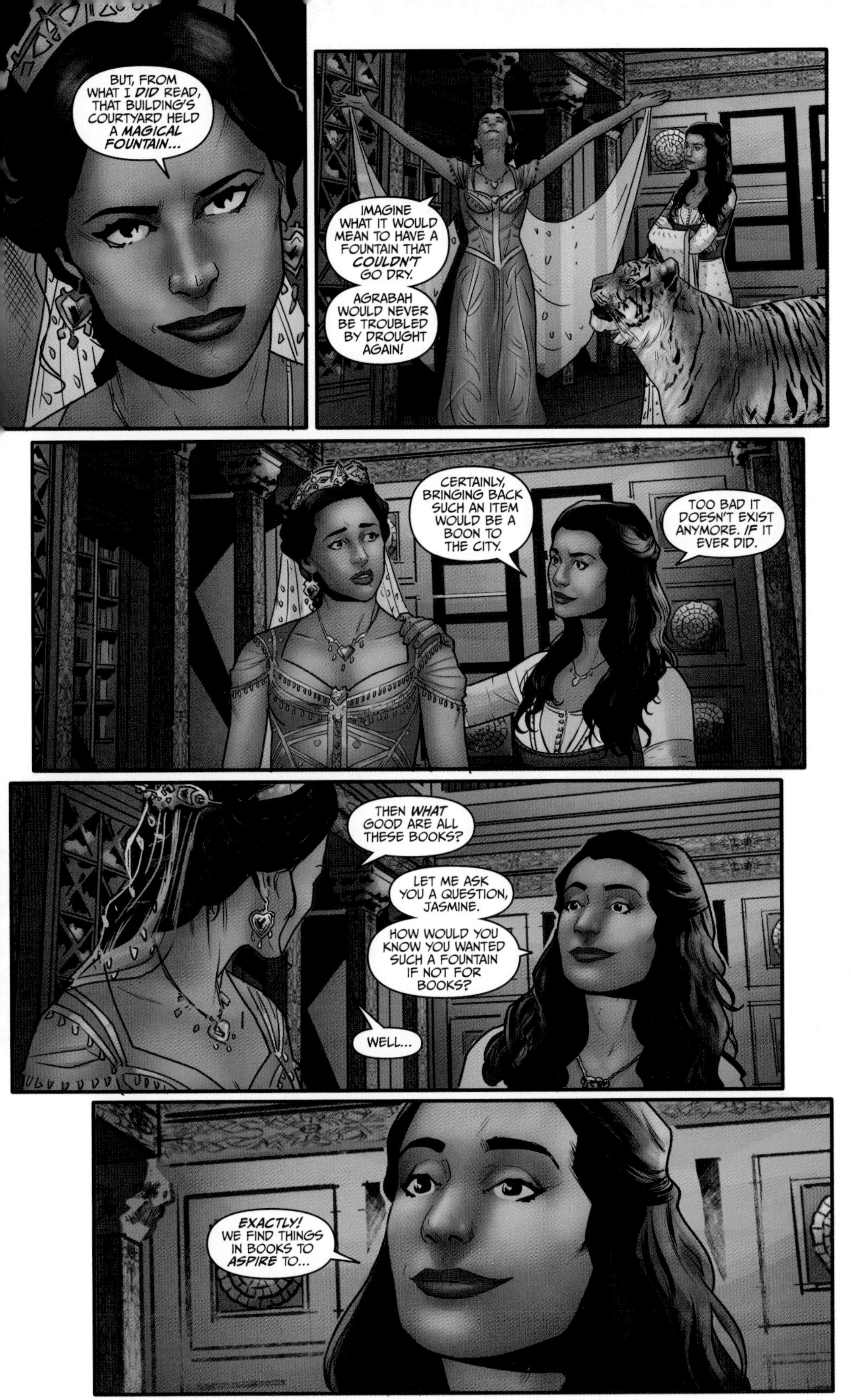
BUT, FROM WHAT I *DID* READ, THAT BUILDING'S COURTYARD HELD A *MAGICAL FOUNTAIN*...
IMAGINE WHAT IT WOULD MEAN TO HAVE A FOUNTAIN THAT *COULDN'T* GO DRY.
AGRABAH WOULD NEVER BE TROUBLED BY DROUGHT AGAIN!
CERTAINLY, BRINGING BACK SUCH AN ITEM WOULD BE A BOON TO THE CITY.
TOO BAD IT DOESN'T EXIST ANYMORE. *IF* IT EVER DID.
THEN *WHAT* GOOD ARE ALL THESE BOOKS?
LET ME ASK YOU A QUESTION, JASMINE.
HOW WOULD YOU KNOW YOU WANTED SUCH A FOUNTAIN IF NOT FOR BOOKS?
WELL...
EXACTLY! WE FIND THINGS IN BOOKS TO *ASPIRE* TO...

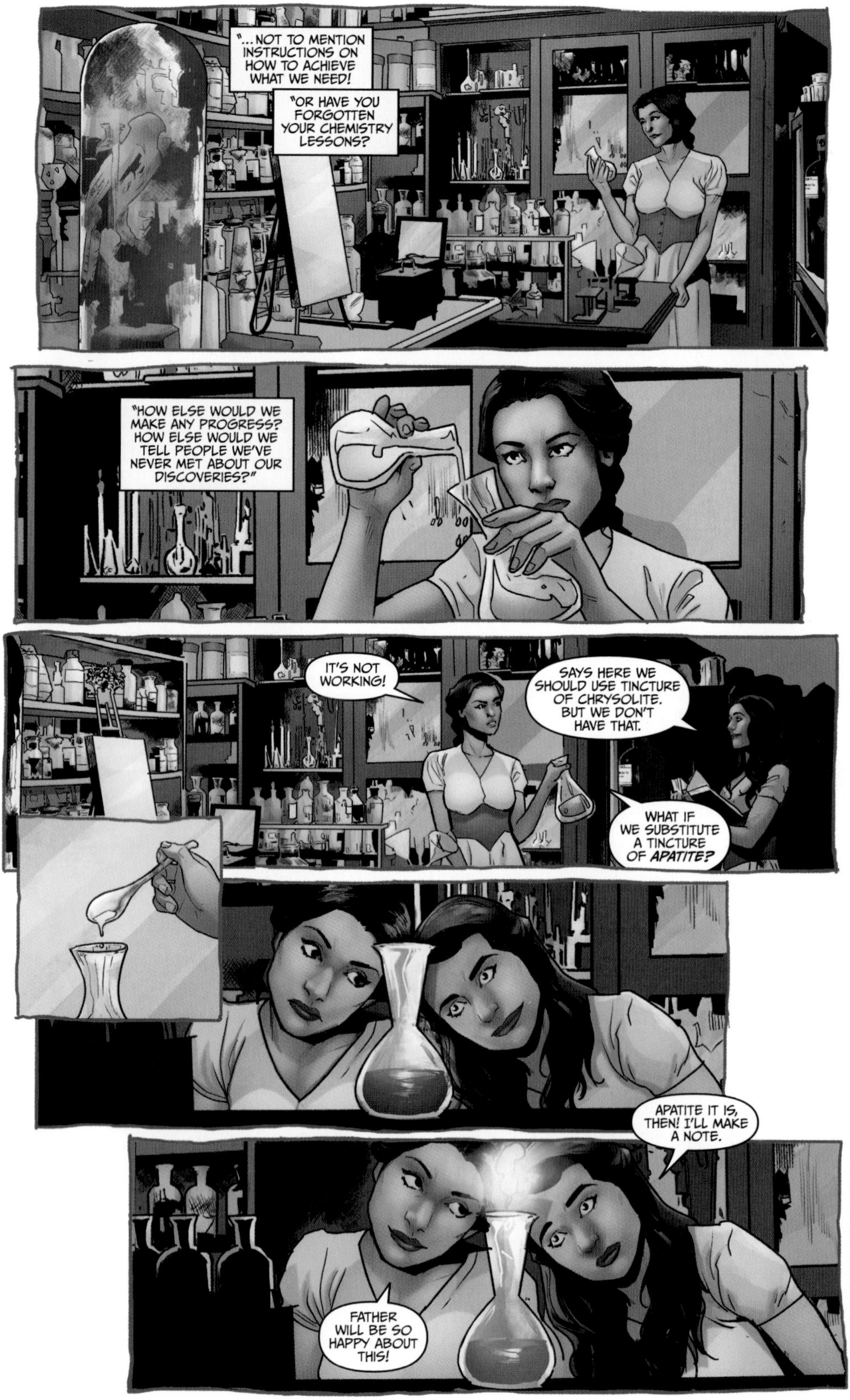
"...NOT TO MENTION INSTRUCTIONS ON HOW TO ACHIEVE WHAT WE NEED!
"OR HAVE YOU FORGOTTEN YOUR CHEMISTRY LESSONS?
"HOW ELSE WOULD WE MAKE ANY PROGRESS? HOW ELSE WOULD WE TELL PEOPLE WE'VE NEVER MET ABOUT OUR DISCOVERIES?"
IT'S NOT WORKING!
SAYS HERE WE SHOULD USE TINCTURE OF CHRYSOLITE. BUT WE DON'T HAVE THAT.
WHAT IF WE SUBSTITUTE A TINCTURE OF *APATITE?*
APATITE IT IS, THEN! I'LL MAKE A NOTE.
FATHER WILL BE SO HAPPY ABOUT THIS!

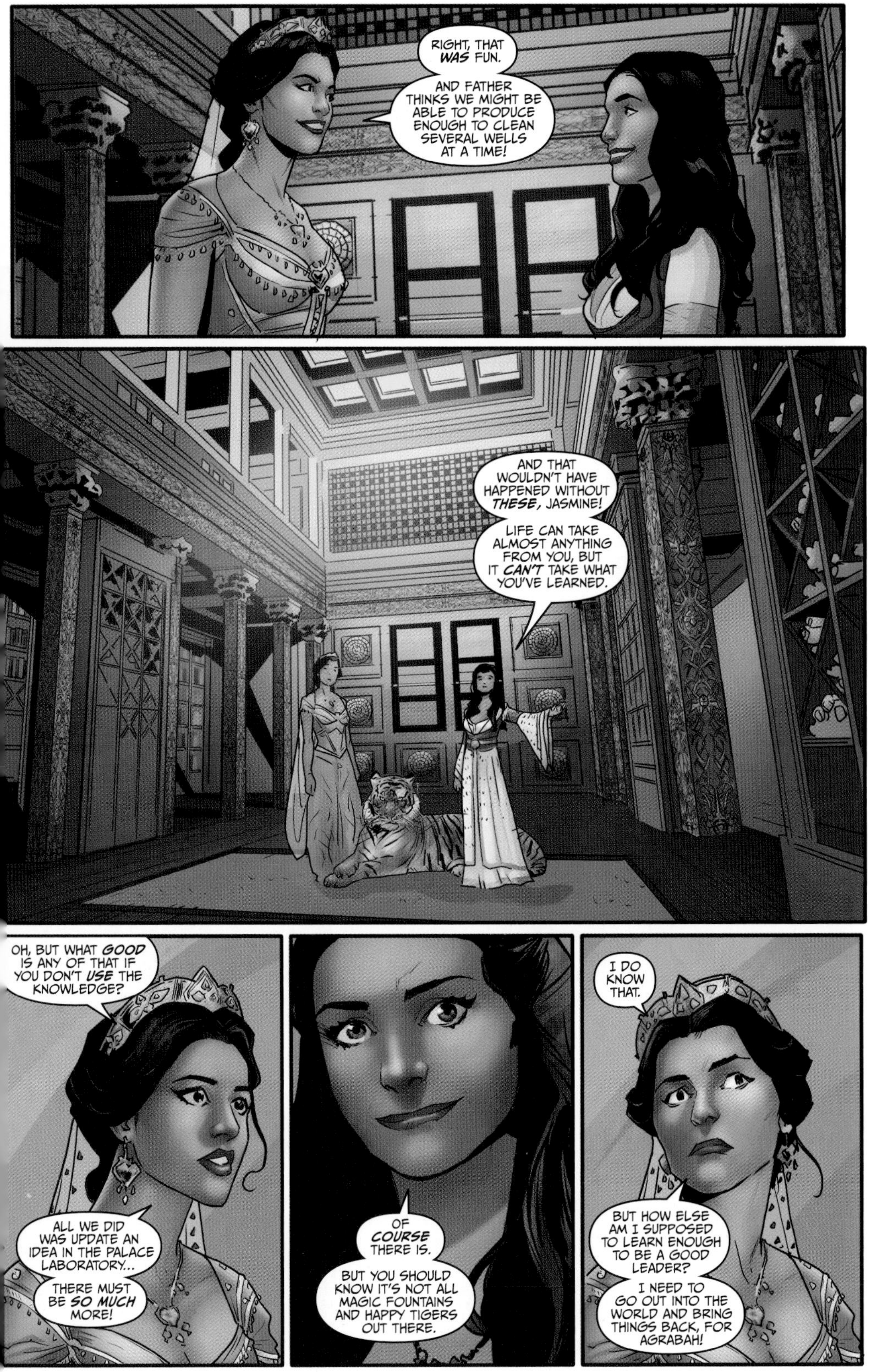
RIGHT, THAT WAS FUN.
AND FATHER THINKS WE MIGHT BE ABLE TO PRODUCE ENOUGH TO CLEAN SEVERAL WELLS AT A TIME!
AND THAT WOULDN'T HAVE HAPPENED WITHOUT THESE, JASMINE!
LIFE CAN TAKE ALMOST ANYTHING FROM YOU, BUT IT CAN'T TAKE WHAT YOU'VE LEARNED.
OH, BUT WHAT GOOD IS ANY OF THAT IF YOU DON'T USE THE KNOWLEDGE?
ALL WE DID WAS UPDATE AN IDEA IN THE PALACE LABORATORY...
THERE MUST BE SO MUCH MORE!
OF COURSE THERE IS.
BUT YOU SHOULD KNOW IT'S NOT ALL MAGIC FOUNTAINS AND HAPPY TIGERS OUT THERE.
I DO KNOW THAT.
BUT HOW ELSE AM I SUPPOSED TO LEARN ENOUGH TO BE A GOOD LEADER?
I NEED TO GO OUT INTO THE WORLD AND BRING THINGS BACK, FOR AGRABAH!

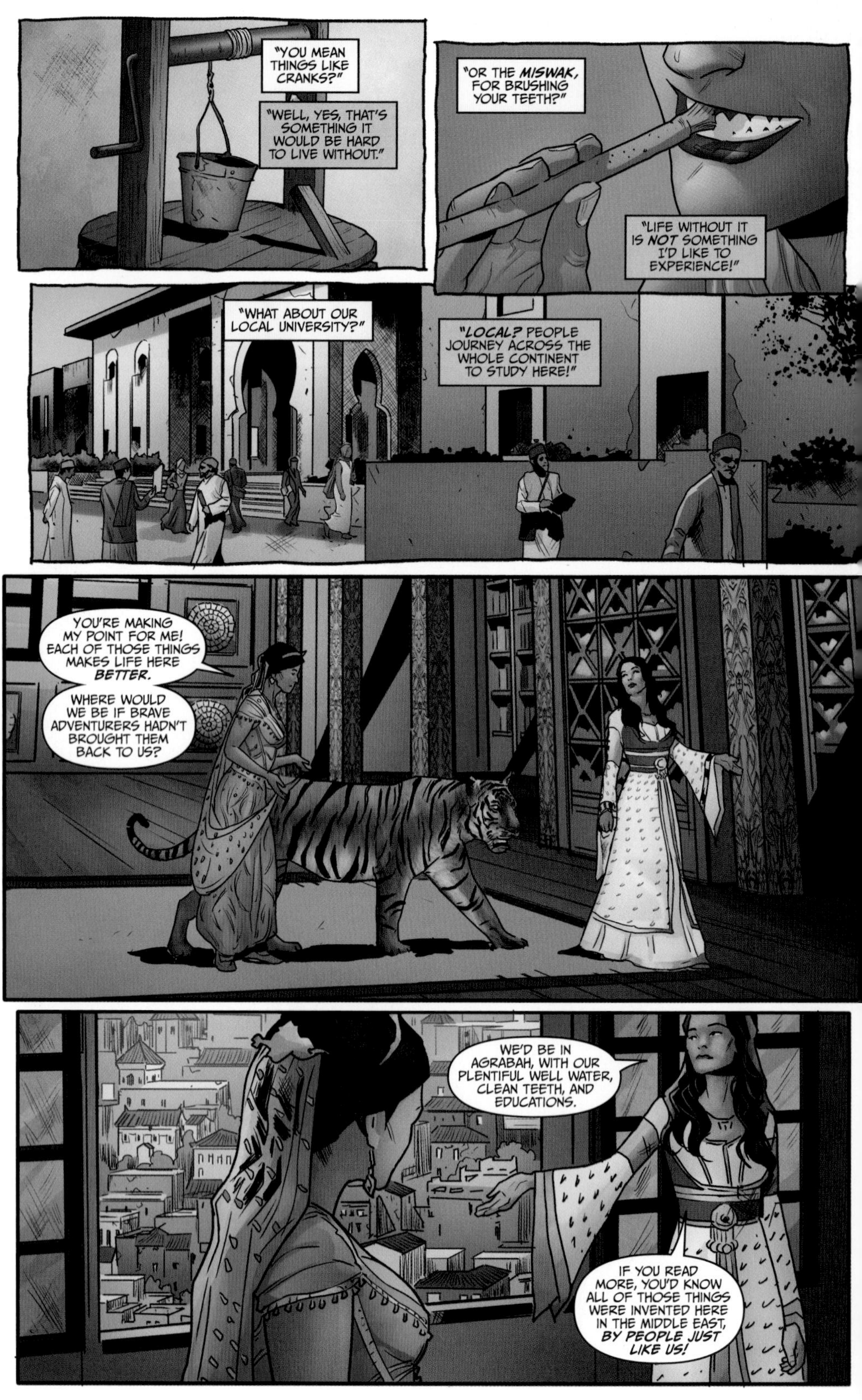
"YOU MEAN THINGS LIKE CRANKS?"
"WELL, YES, THAT'S SOMETHING IT WOULD BE HARD TO LIVE WITHOUT."
"OR THE MISWAK, FOR BRUSHING YOUR TEETH?"
"LIFE WITHOUT IT IS NOT SOMETHING I'D LIKE TO EXPERIENCE!"
"WHAT ABOUT OUR LOCAL UNIVERSITY?"
"LOCAL? PEOPLE JOURNEY ACROSS THE WHOLE CONTINENT TO STUDY HERE!"
YOU'RE MAKING MY POINT FOR ME! EACH OF THOSE THINGS MAKES LIFE HERE BETTER.
WHERE WOULD WE BE IF BRAVE ADVENTURERS HADN'T BROUGHT THEM BACK TO US?
WE'D BE IN AGRABAH, WITH OUR PLENTIFUL WELL WATER, CLEAN TEETH, AND EDUCATIONS.
IF YOU READ MORE, YOU'D KNOW ALL OF THOSE THINGS WERE INVENTED HERE IN THE MIDDLE EAST, BY PEOPLE JUST LIKE US!

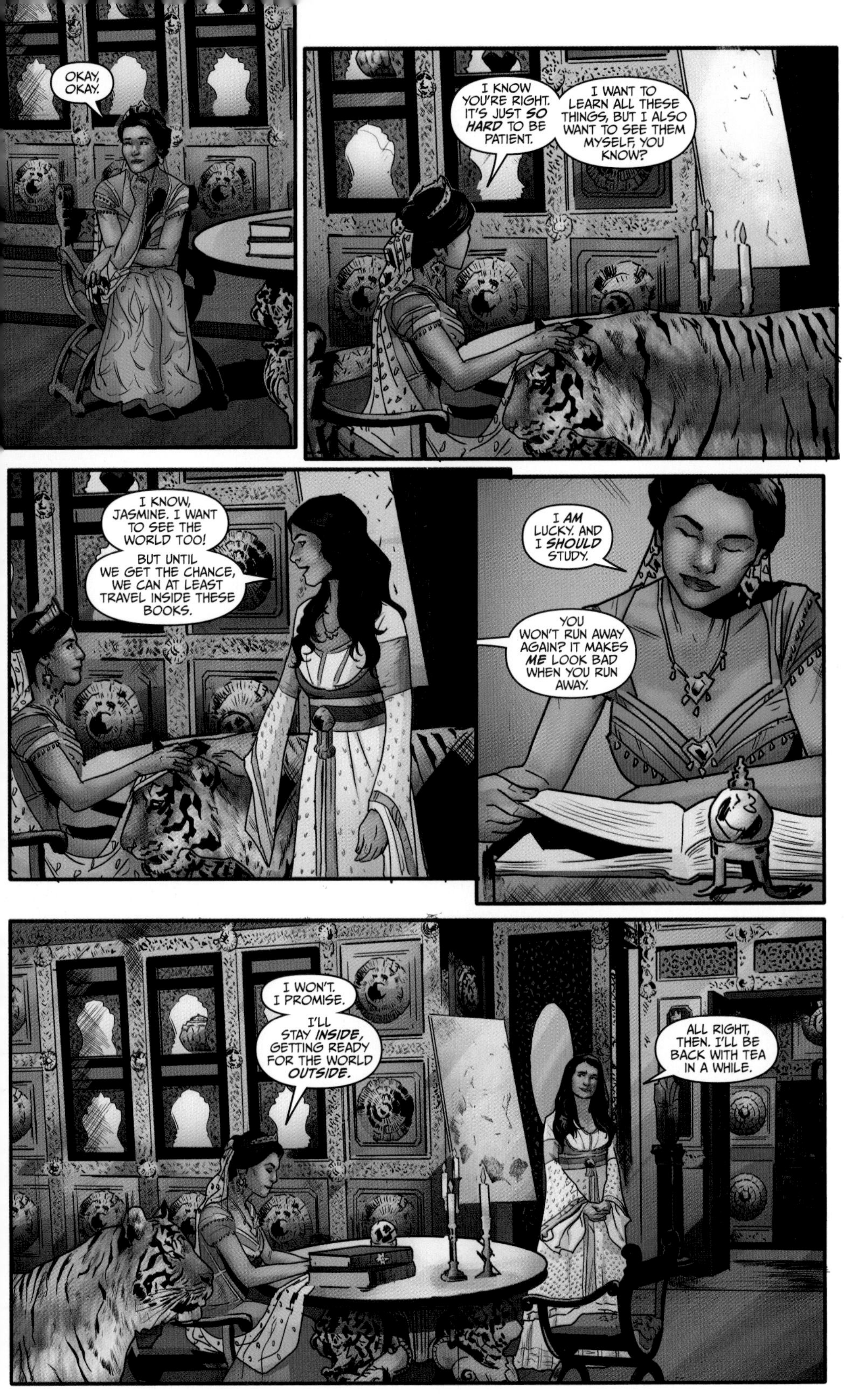

OKAY, OKAY.
I KNOW YOU'RE RIGHT. IT'S JUST SO HARD TO BE PATIENT.
I WANT TO LEARN ALL THESE THINGS, BUT I ALSO WANT TO SEE THEM MYSELF, YOU KNOW?
I KNOW, JASMINE. I WANT TO SEE THE WORLD TOO!
BUT UNTIL WE GET THE CHANCE, WE CAN AT LEAST TRAVEL INSIDE THESE BOOKS.
I AM LUCKY. AND I SHOULD STUDY.
YOU WON'T RUN AWAY AGAIN? IT MAKES ME LOOK BAD WHEN YOU RUN AWAY.
I WON'T. I PROMISE.
I'LL STAY INSIDE, GETTING READY FOR THE WORLD OUTSIDE.
ALL RIGHT, THEN. I'LL BE BACK WITH TEA IN A WHILE.

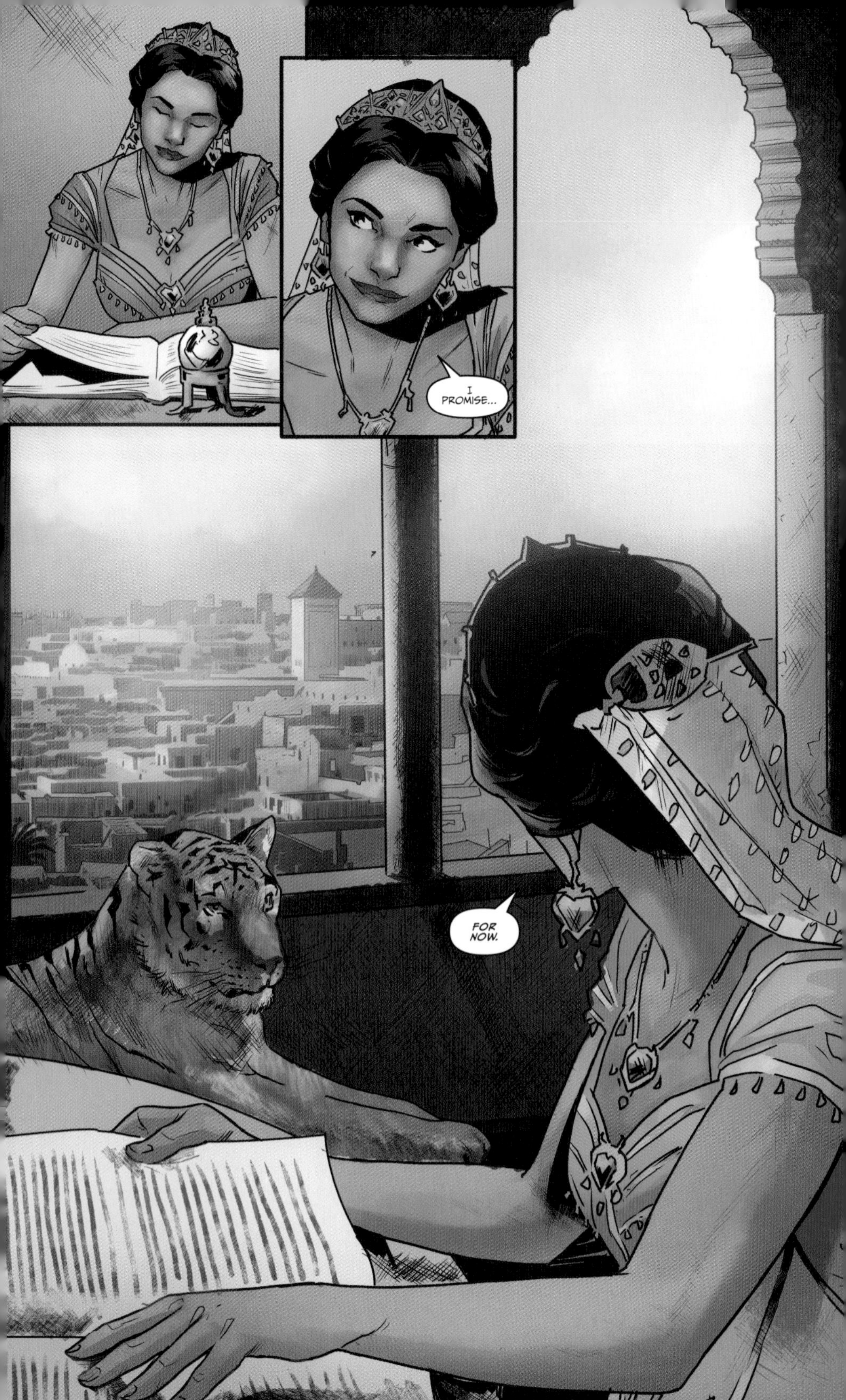
I PROMISE...
FOR NOW.

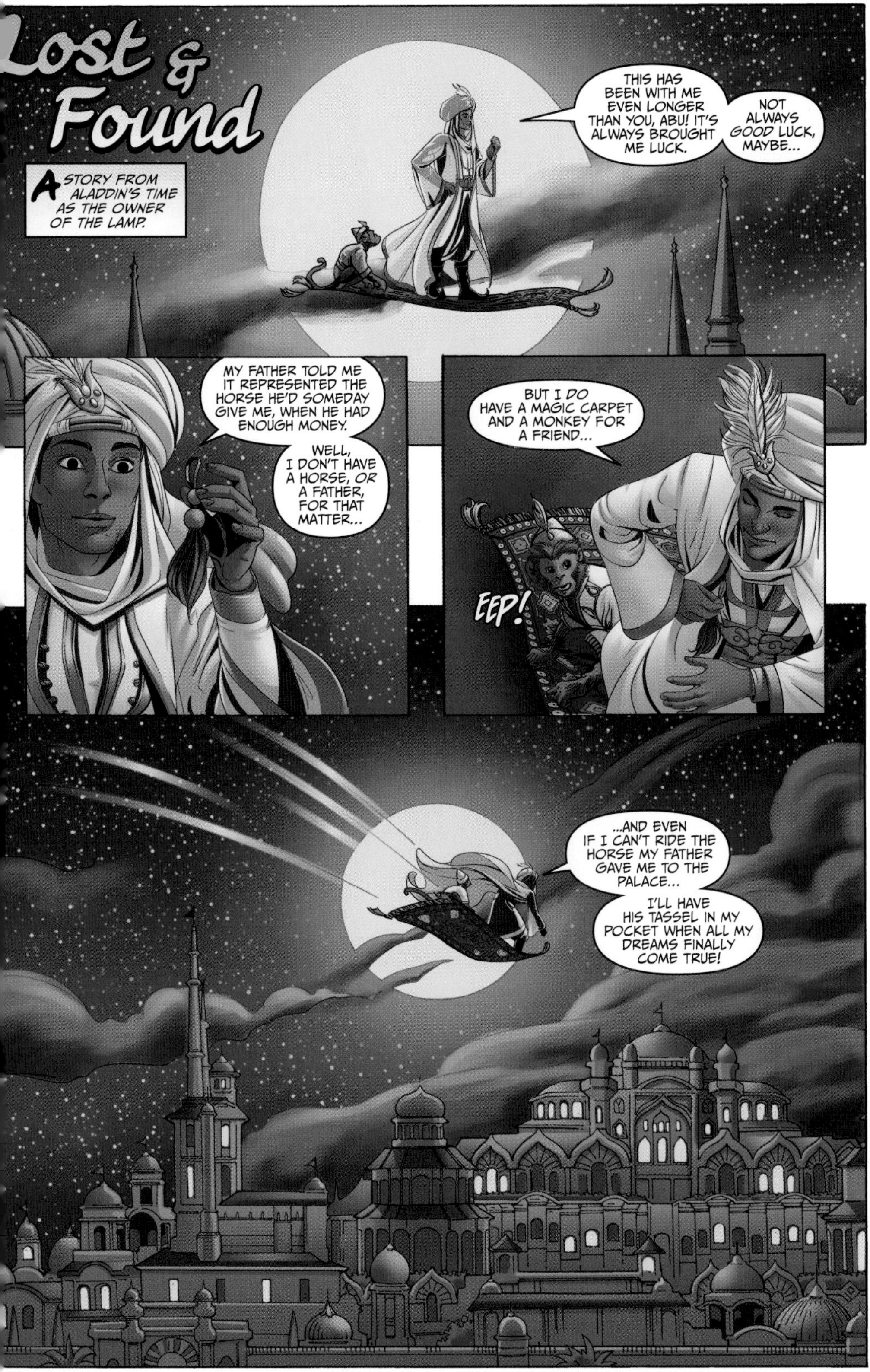
Lost & Found
A STORY FROM ALADDIN'S TIME AS THE OWNER OF THE LAMP.
THIS HAS BEEN WITH ME EVEN LONGER THAN YOU, ABU! IT'S ALWAYS BROUGHT ME LUCK.
NOT ALWAYS GOOD LUCK, MAYBE...
MY FATHER TOLD ME IT REPRESENTED THE HORSE HE'D SOMEDAY GIVE ME, WHEN HE HAD ENOUGH MONEY.
WELL, I DON'T HAVE A HORSE, OR A FATHER, FOR THAT MATTER...
BUT I DO HAVE A MAGIC CARPET AND A MONKEY FOR A FRIEND...
EEP!
...AND EVEN IF I CAN'T RIDE THE HORSE MY FATHER GAVE ME TO THE PALACE...
I'LL HAVE HIS TASSEL IN MY POCKET WHEN ALL MY DREAMS FINALLY COME TRUE!

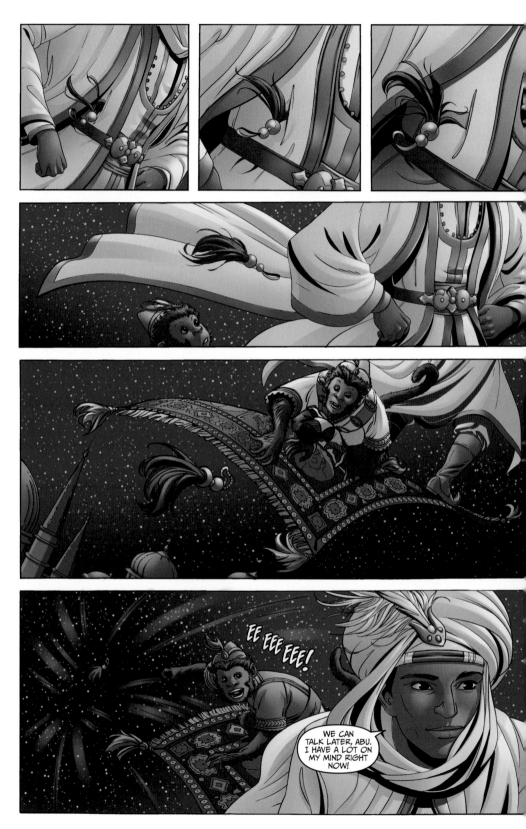

EE EEE EEE!

WE CAN TALK LATER, ABU. I HAVE A LOT ON MY MIND RIGHT NOW!

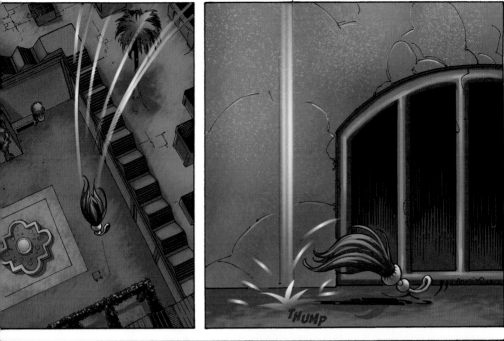

THUMP

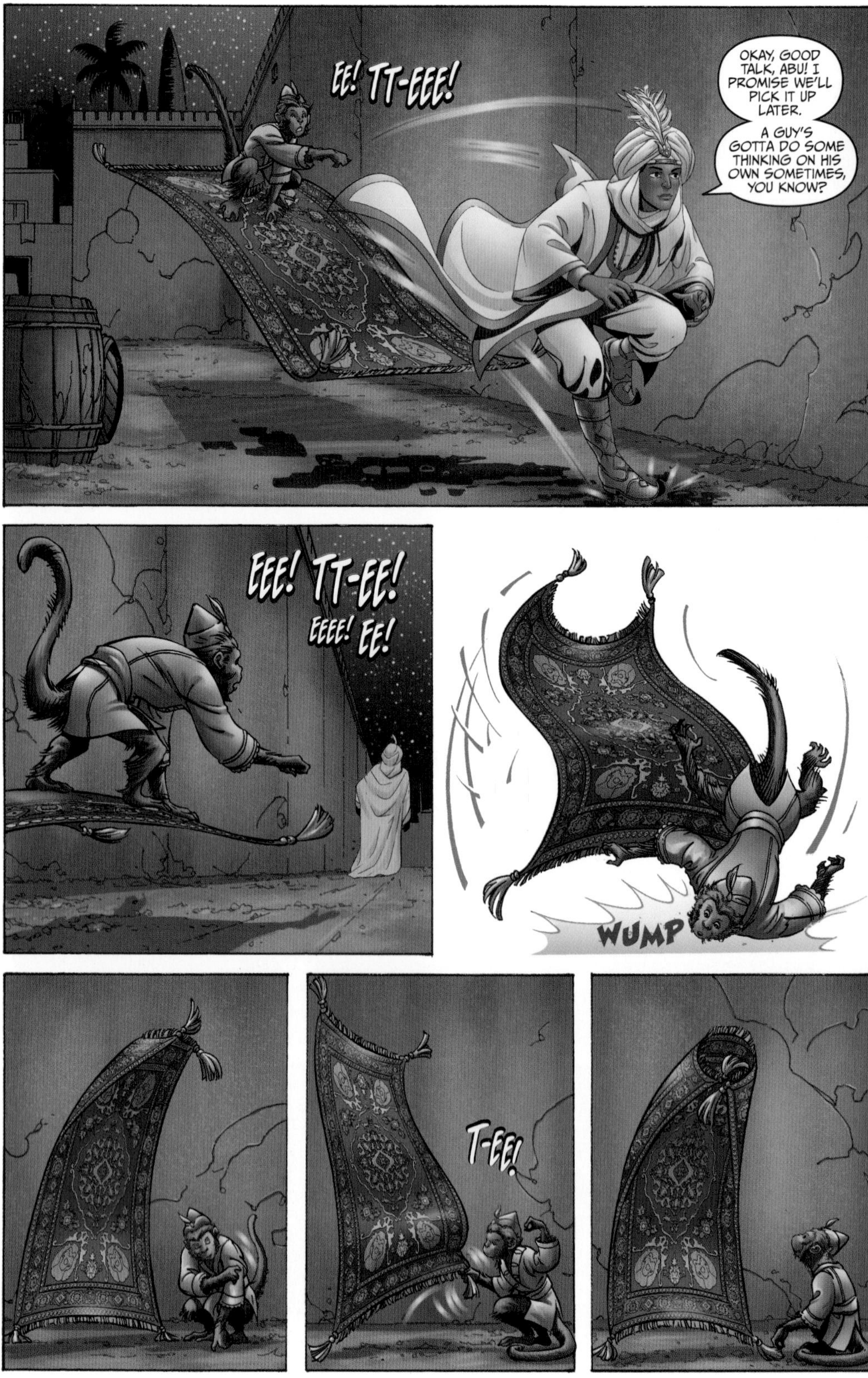
EE! TT-EEE!
OKAY, GOOD TALK, ABU! I PROMISE WE'LL PICK IT UP LATER.
A GUY'S GOTTA DO SOME THINKING ON HIS OWN SOMETIMES, YOU KNOW?
EEE! TT-EE!
EEEE! EE!
WUMP
T-EE!

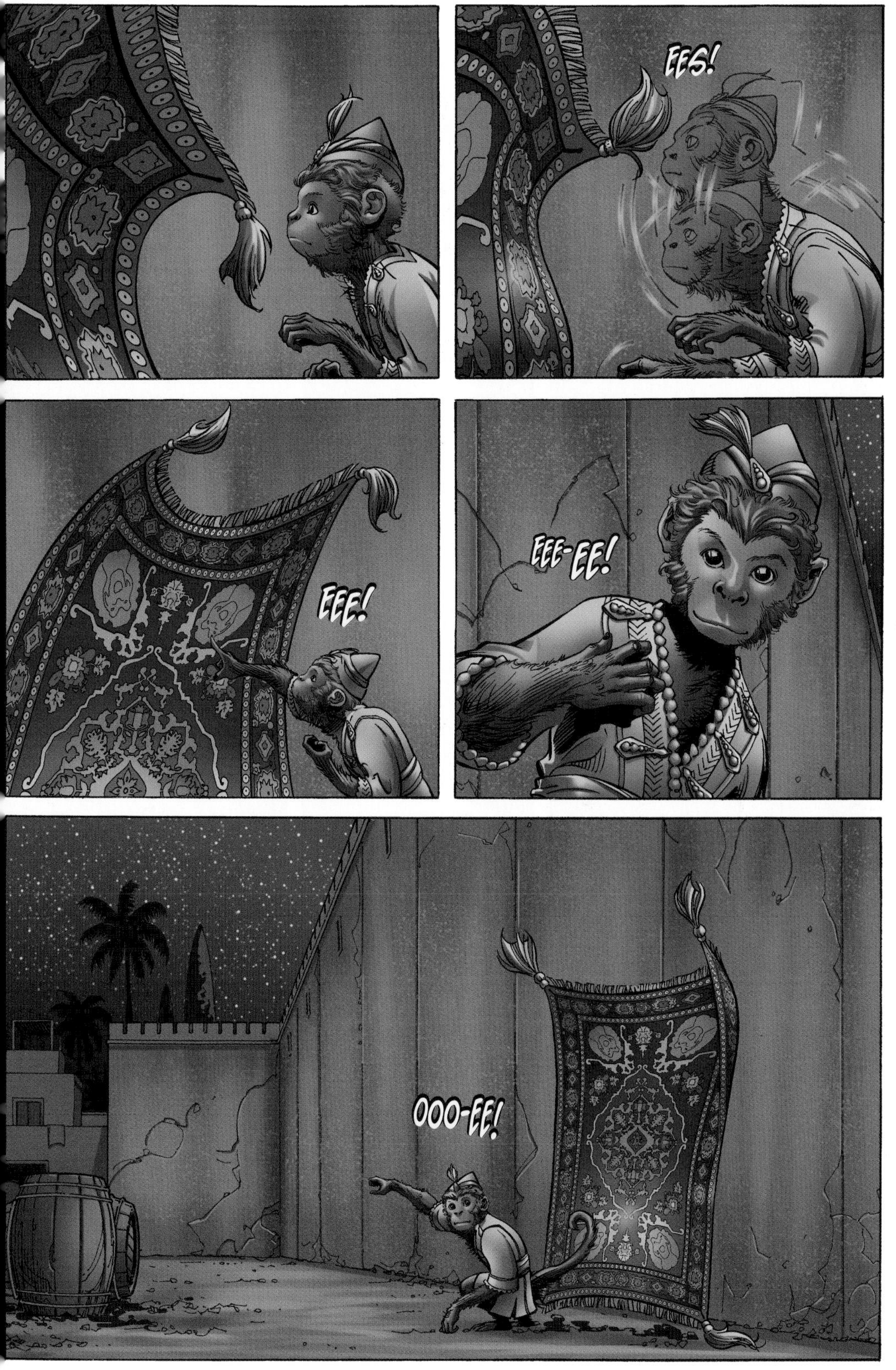
EES!
EEE!
EEE-EE!
OOO-EE!

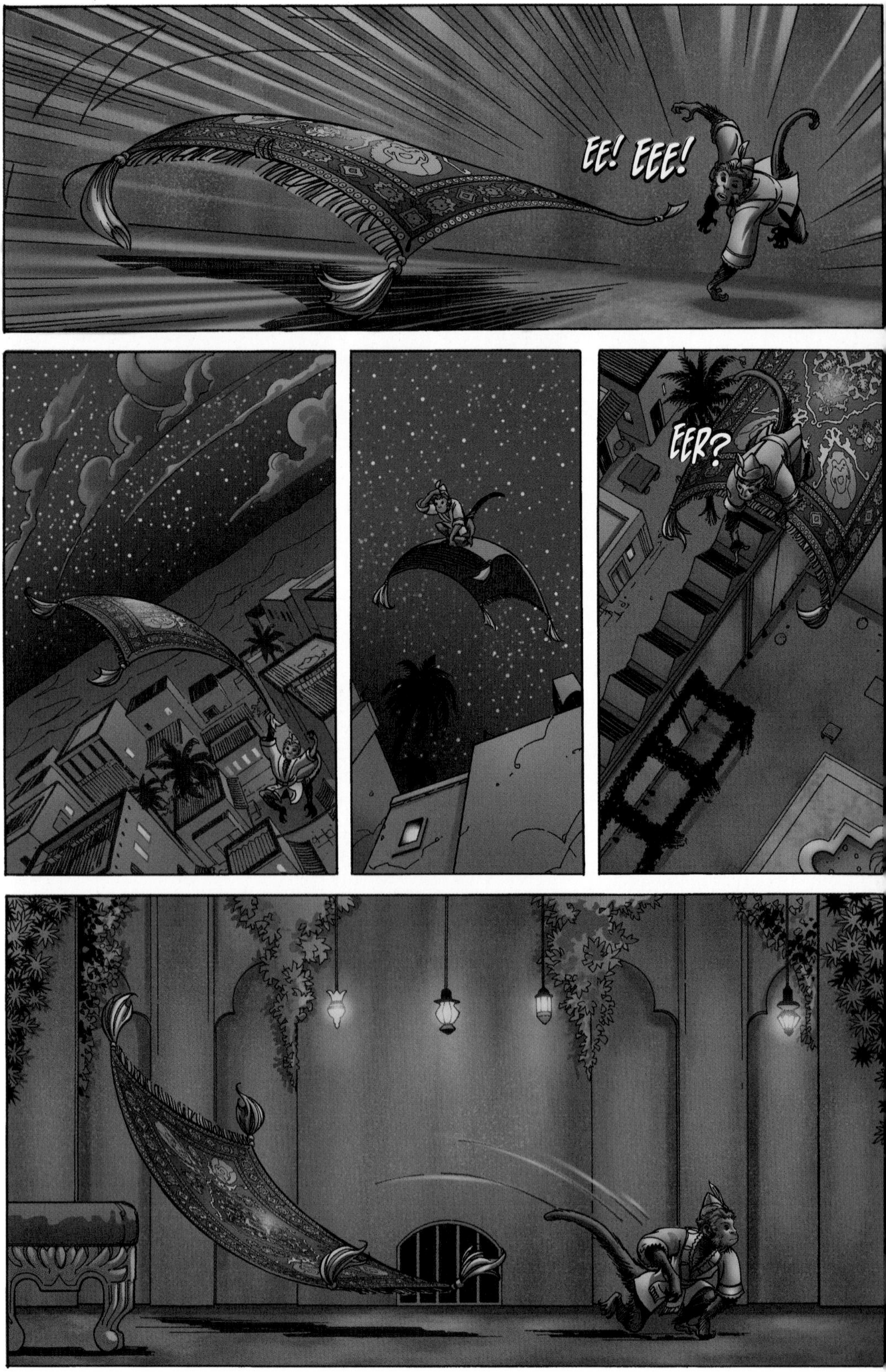
EE! EEE!
EER?

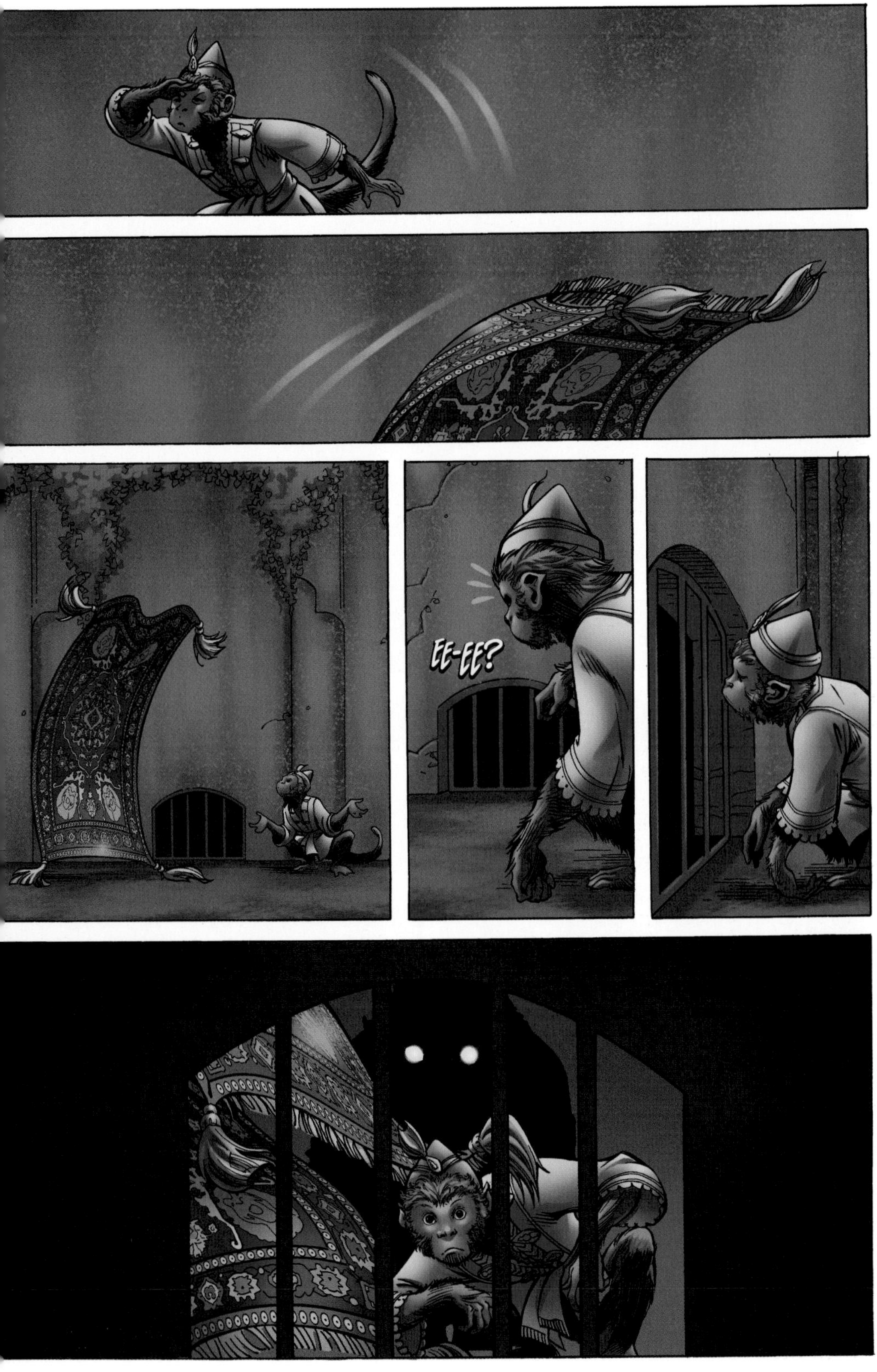
EE-EE?

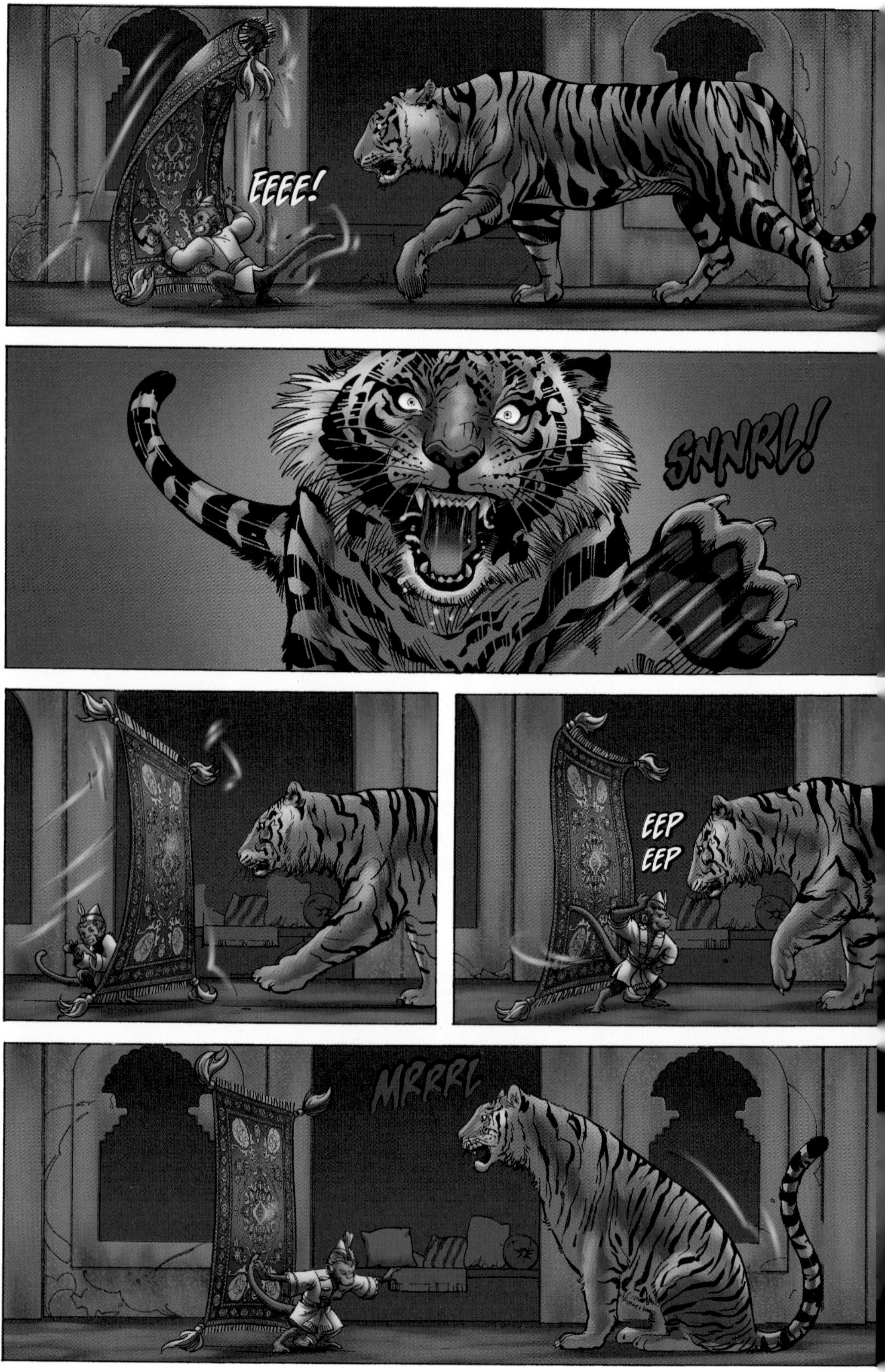
EEEE!
SNNRL!
EEP
EEP
MRRRL

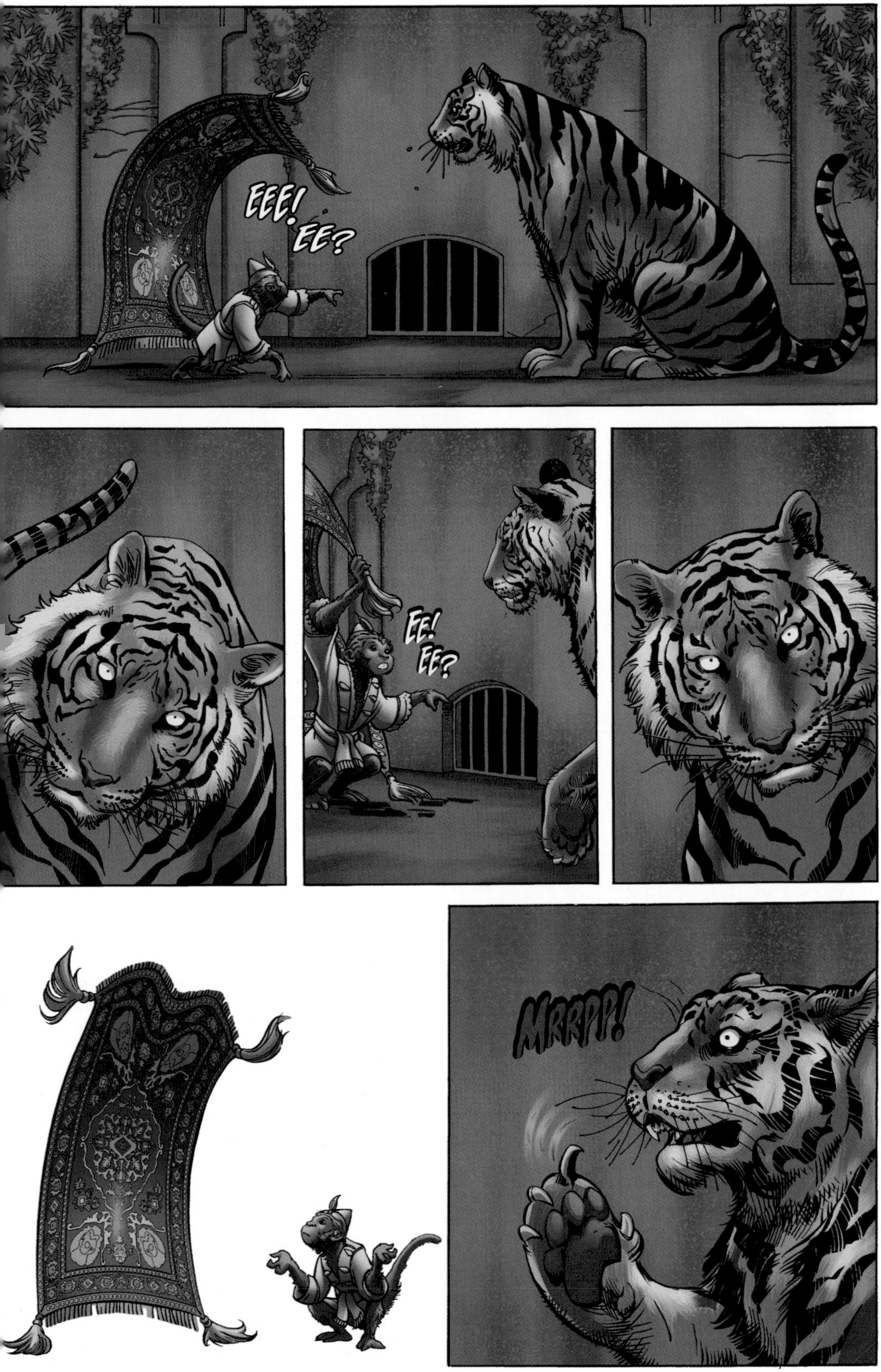
EEE!
EE?
EE!
EE?
MRRPP!

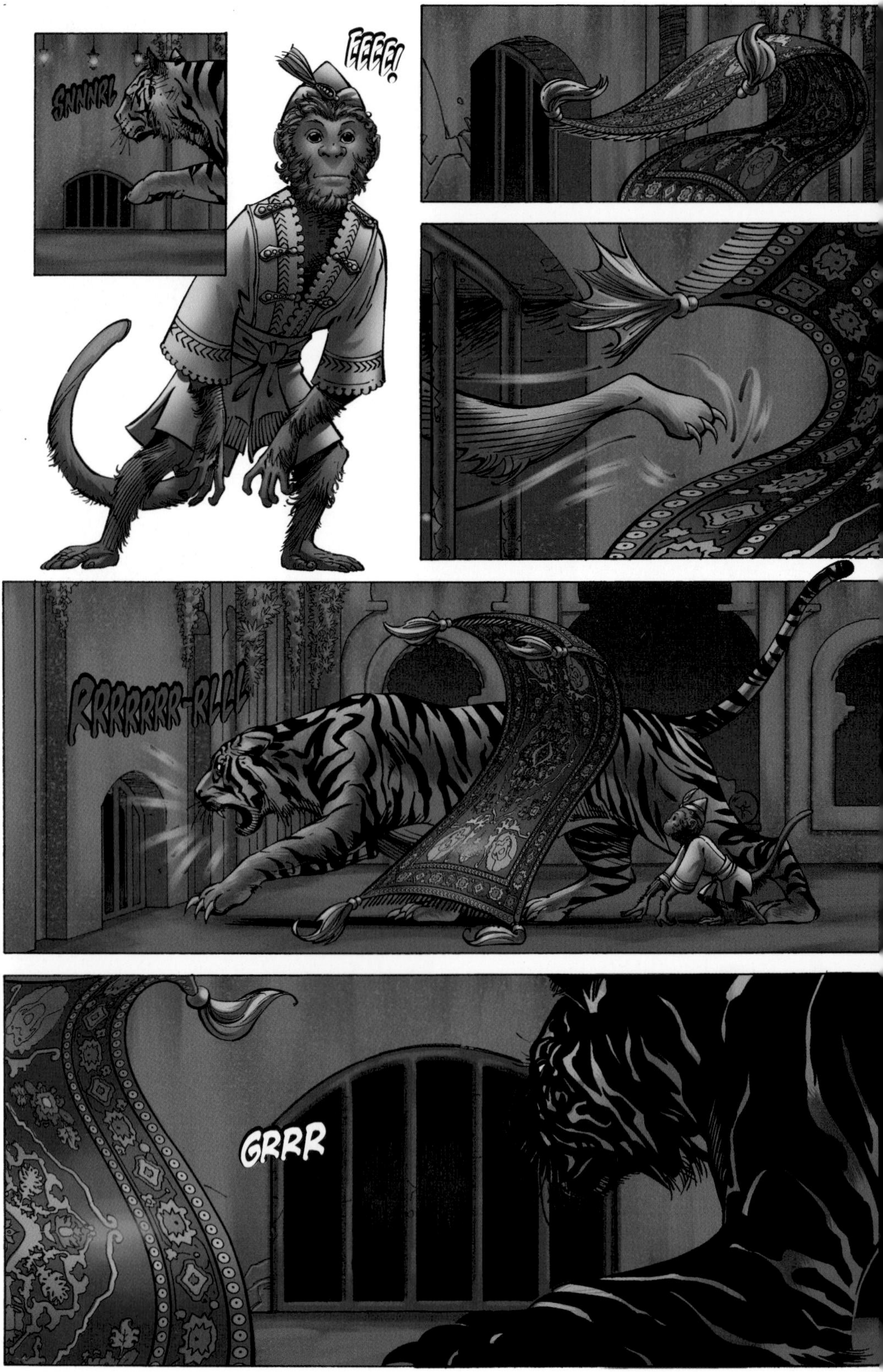
SNNNRL
EEEE!
RRRRRRR-RLLL
GRRR

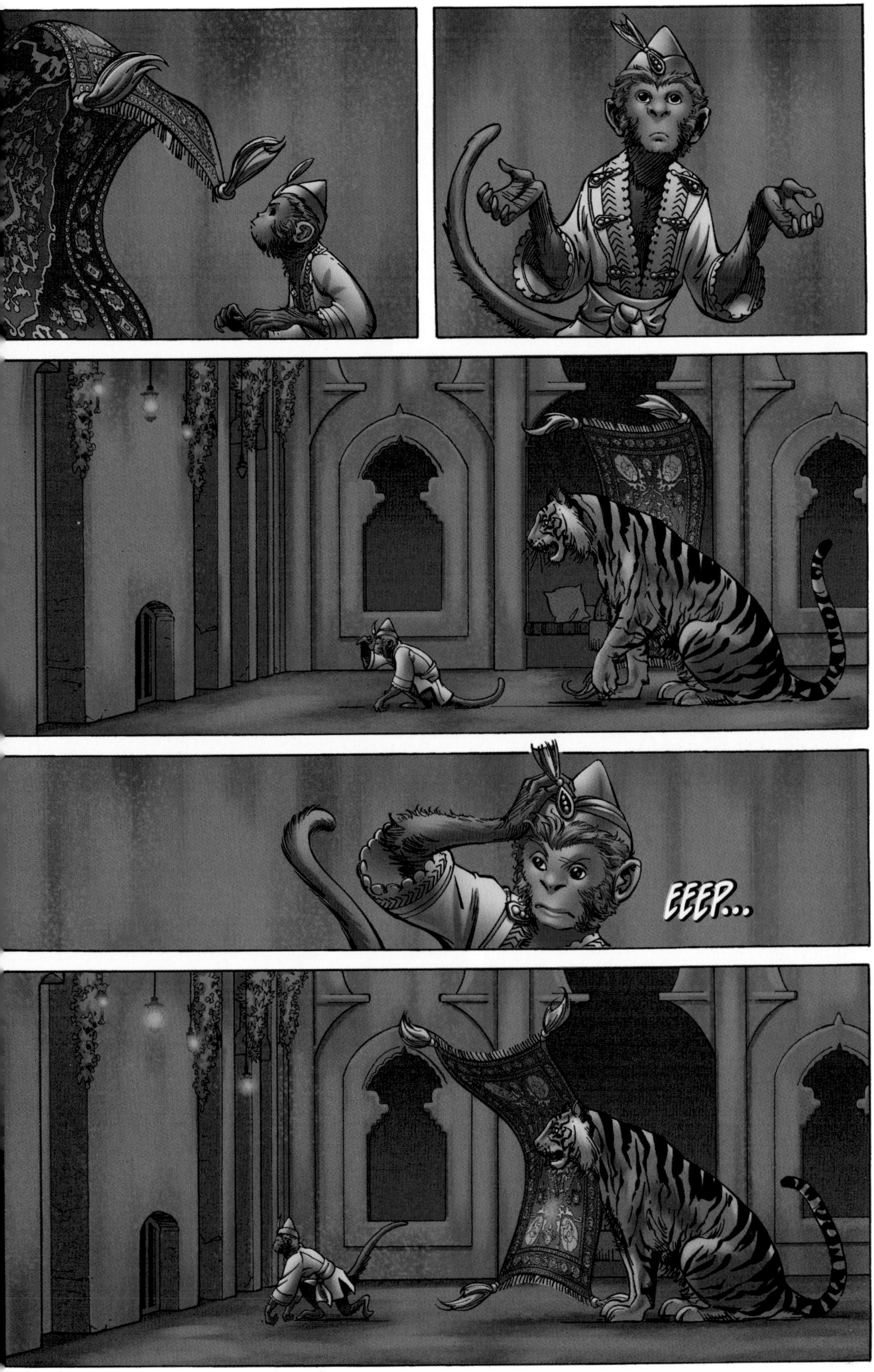
EEEP...

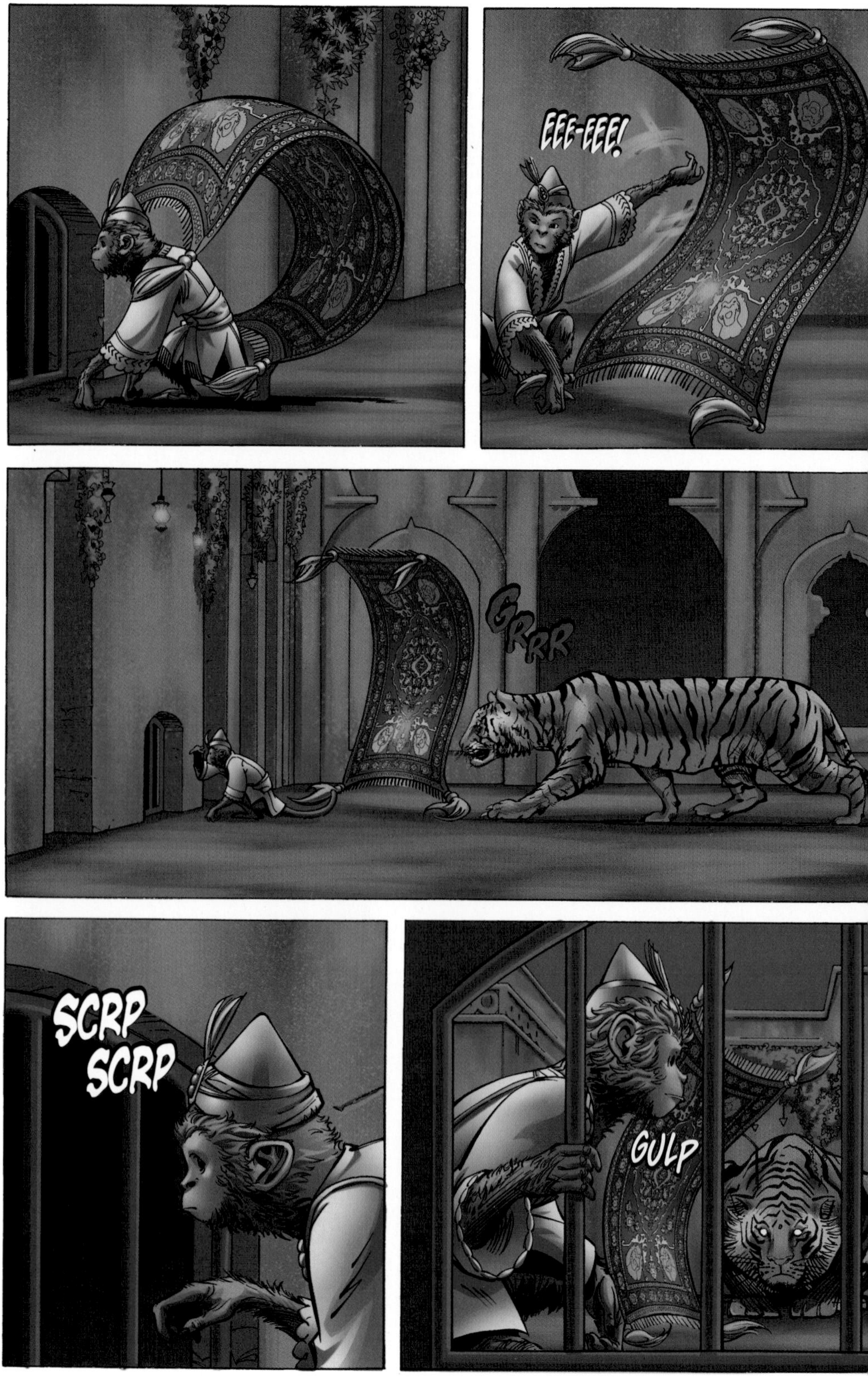
EEE-EEE!
GRRR
SCRP
SCRP
GULP

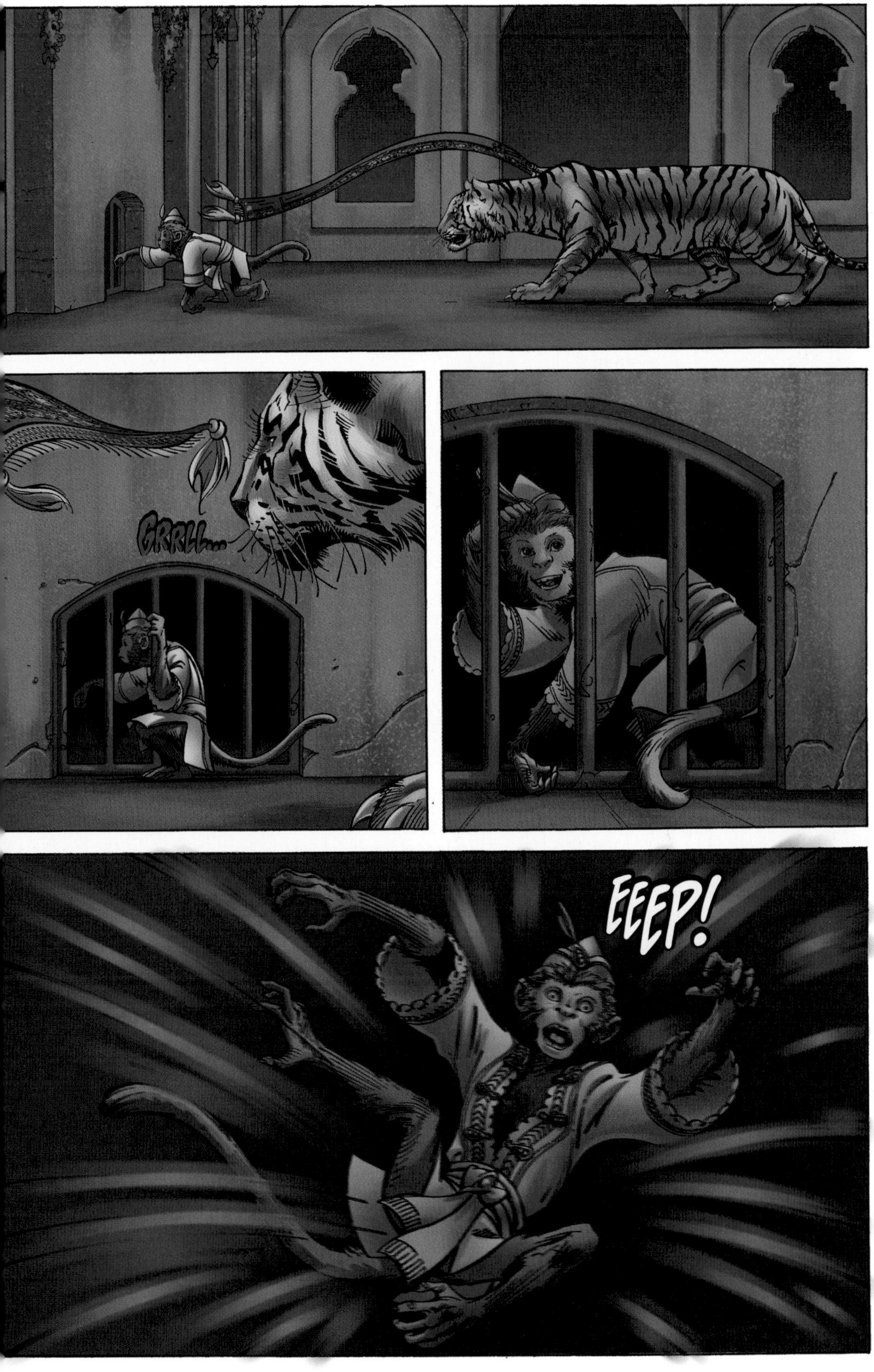
GRRLL...
EEEP!

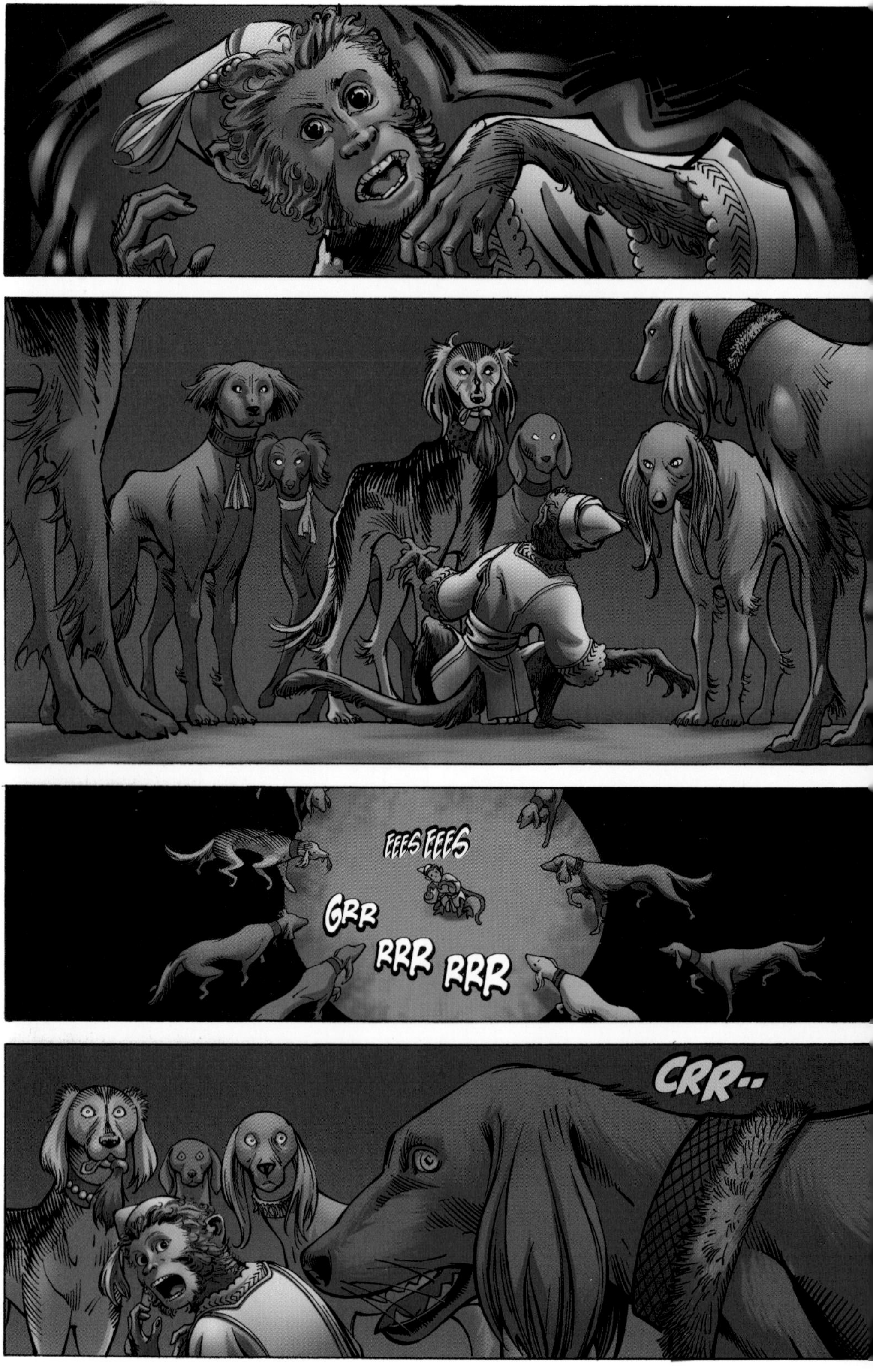
EEES EEES
GRR
RRR RRR
CRR..

CRAK!
RAAWR!
WHIMPER
OOOOO
GRR
EE!

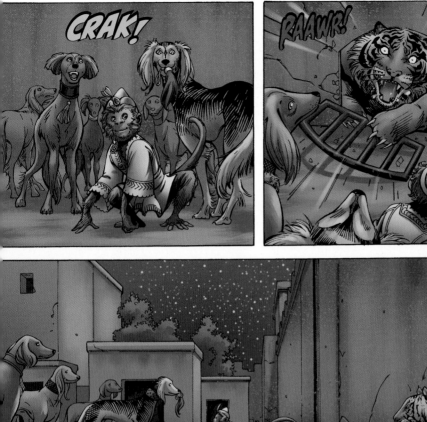

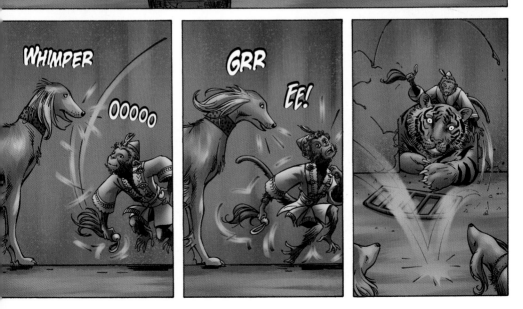

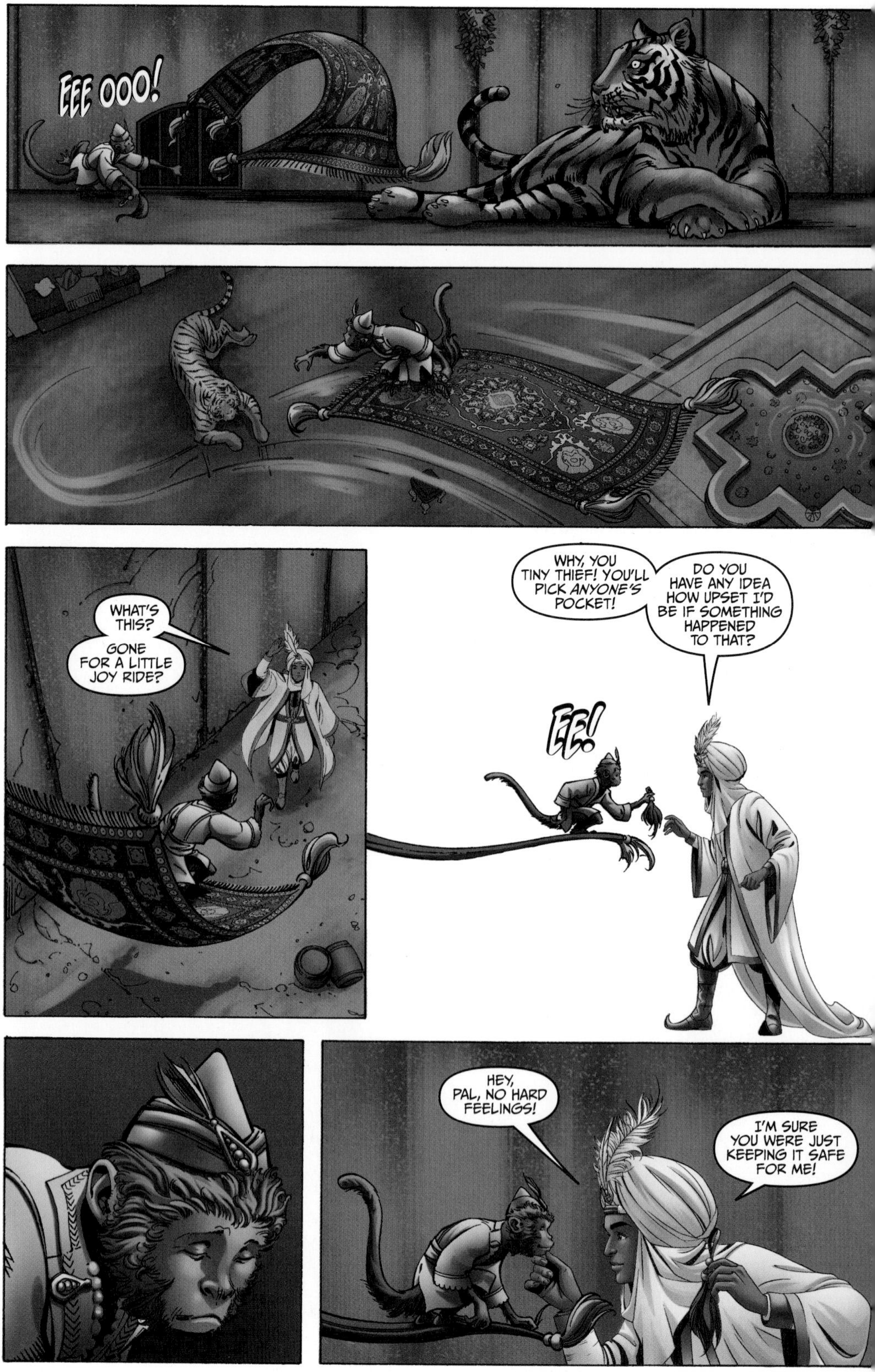
EEE OOO!
WHAT'S THIS?
GONE FOR A LITTLE JOY RIDE?
WHY, YOU TINY THIEF! YOU'LL PICK ANYONE'S POCKET!
DO YOU HAVE ANY IDEA HOW UPSET I'D BE IF SOMETHING HAPPENED TO THAT?
EE!
HEY, PAL, NO HARD FEELINGS!
I'M SURE YOU WERE JUST KEEPING IT SAFE FOR ME!

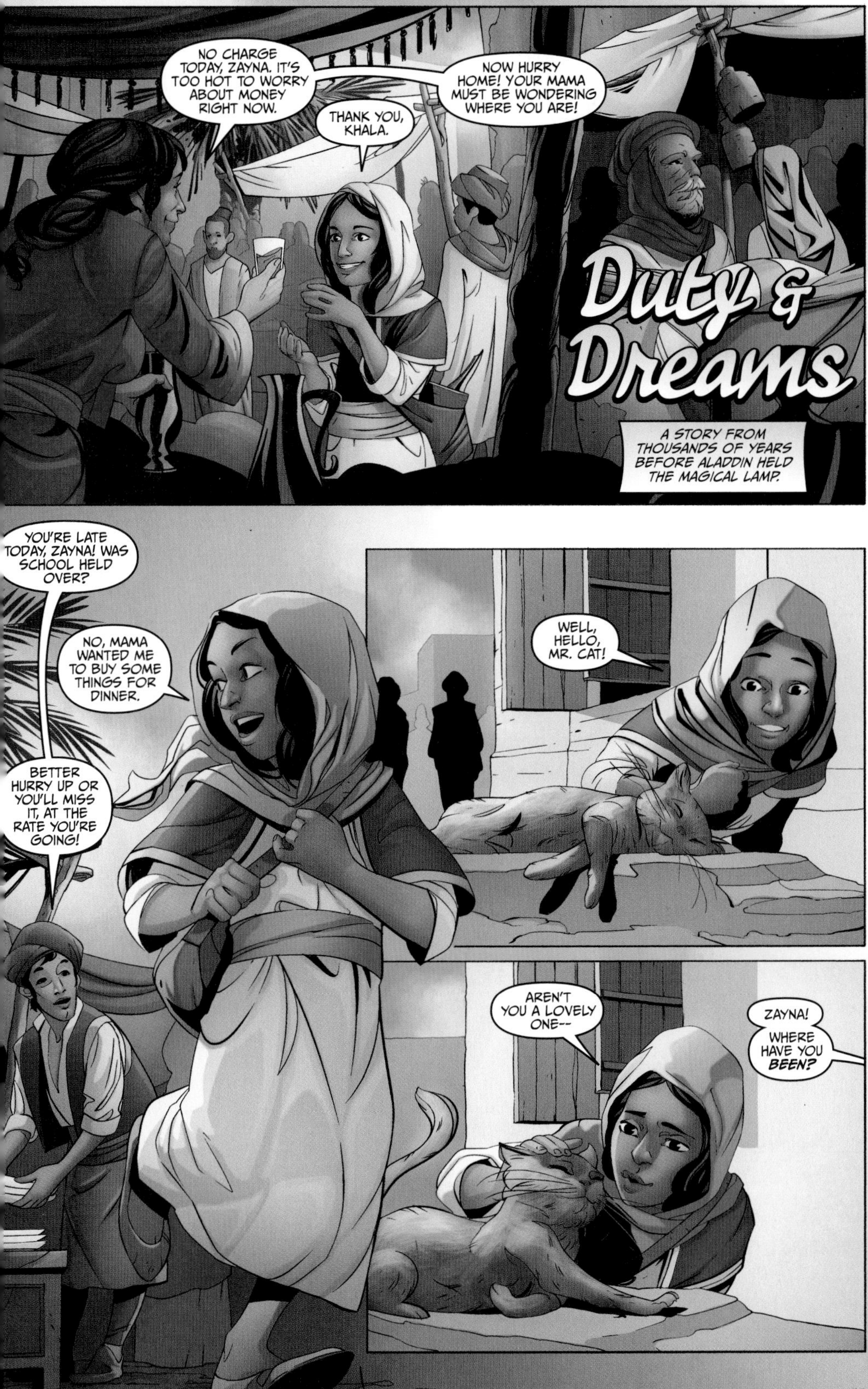
NO CHARGE TODAY, ZAYNA. IT'S TOO HOT TO WORRY ABOUT MONEY RIGHT NOW.
THANK YOU, KHALA.
NOW HURRY HOME! YOUR MAMA MUST BE WONDERING WHERE YOU ARE!
Duty & Dreams
A STORY FROM THOUSANDS OF YEARS BEFORE ALADDIN HELD THE MAGICAL LAMP.
YOU'RE LATE TODAY, ZAYNA! WAS SCHOOL HELD OVER?
NO, MAMA WANTED ME TO BUY SOME THINGS FOR DINNER.
BETTER HURRY UP OR YOU'LL MISS IT, AT THE RATE YOU'RE GOING!
WELL, HELLO, MR. CAT!
AREN'T YOU A LOVELY ONE--
ZAYNA!
WHERE HAVE YOU *BEEN?*

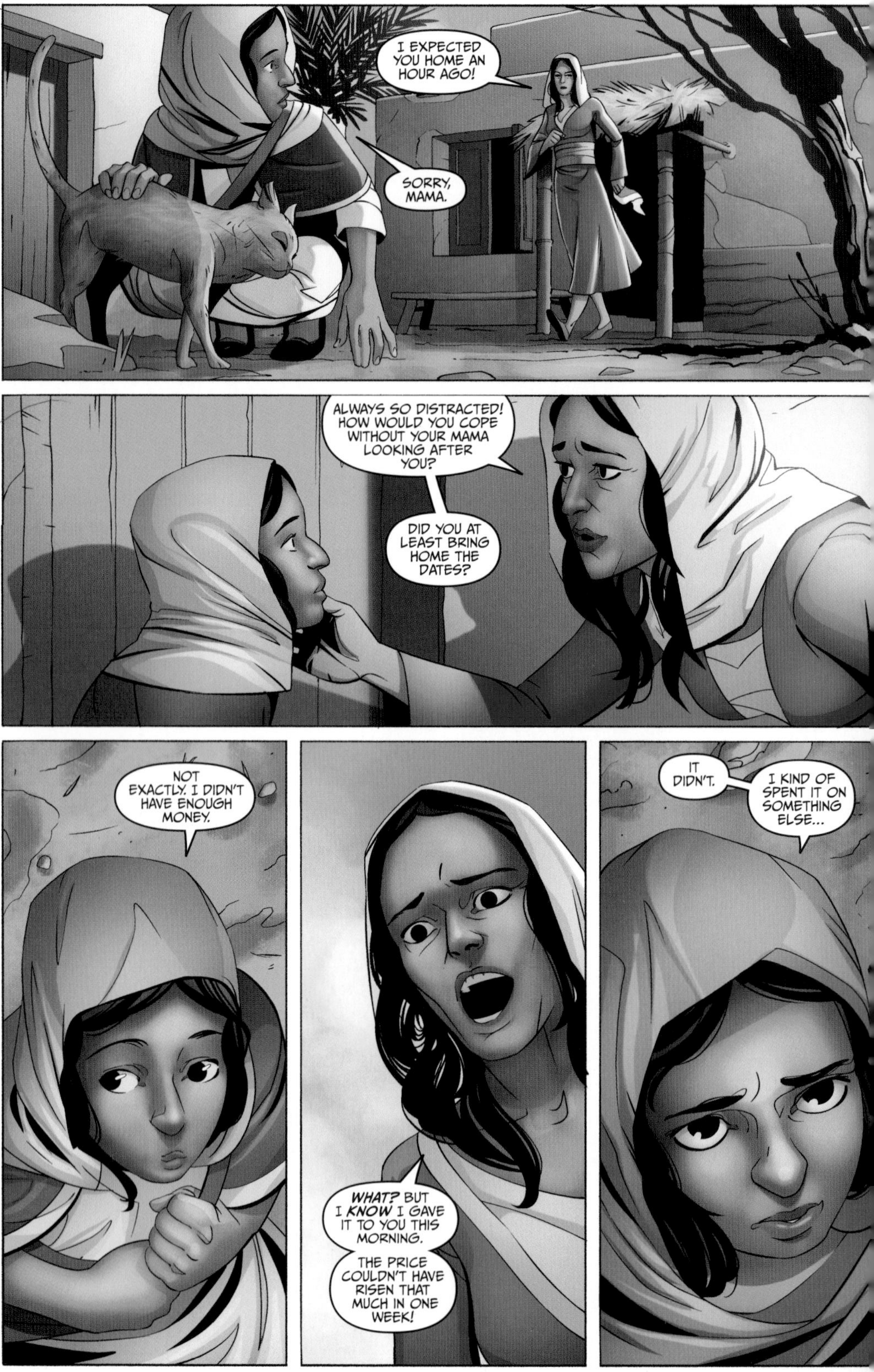
I EXPECTED YOU HOME AN HOUR AGO!
SORRY, MAMA.
ALWAYS SO DISTRACTED! HOW WOULD YOU COPE WITHOUT YOUR MAMA LOOKING AFTER YOU?
DID YOU AT LEAST BRING HOME THE DATES?
NOT EXACTLY. I DIDN'T HAVE ENOUGH MONEY.
WHAT? BUT I KNOW I GAVE IT TO YOU THIS MORNING.
THE PRICE COULDN'T HAVE RISEN THAT MUCH IN ONE WEEK!
IT DIDN'T.
I KIND OF SPENT IT ON SOMETHING ELSE...

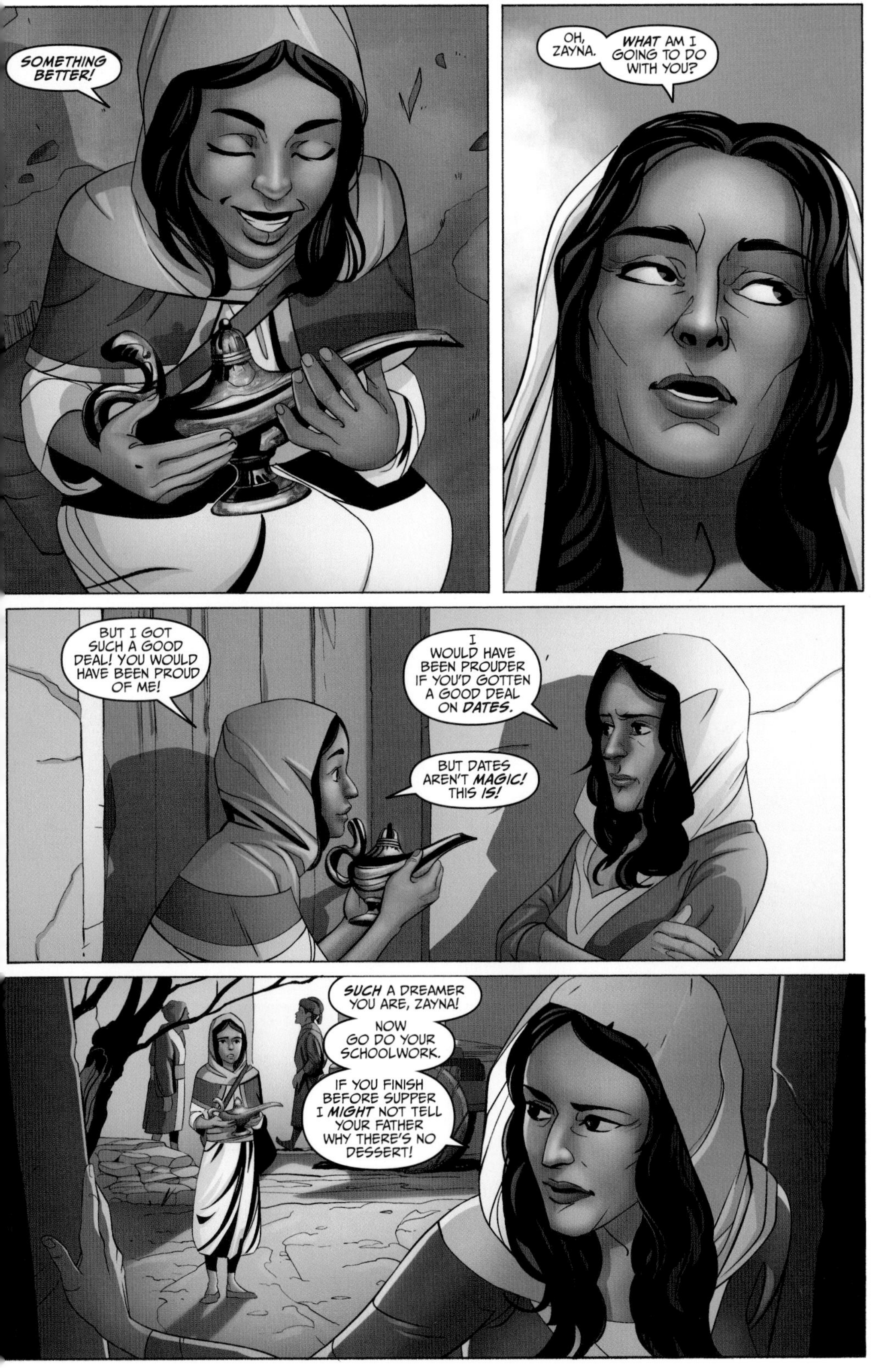
SOMETHING BETTER!
OH, ZAYNA.
WHAT AM I GOING TO DO WITH YOU?
BUT I GOT SUCH A GOOD DEAL! YOU WOULD HAVE BEEN PROUD OF ME!
I WOULD HAVE BEEN PROUDER IF YOU'D GOTTEN A GOOD DEAL ON DATES.
BUT DATES AREN'T MAGIC! THIS IS!
SUCH A DREAMER YOU ARE, ZAYNA!
NOW GO DO YOUR SCHOOLWORK.
IF YOU FINISH BEFORE SUPPER I MIGHT NOT TELL YOUR FATHER WHY THERE'S NO DESSERT!

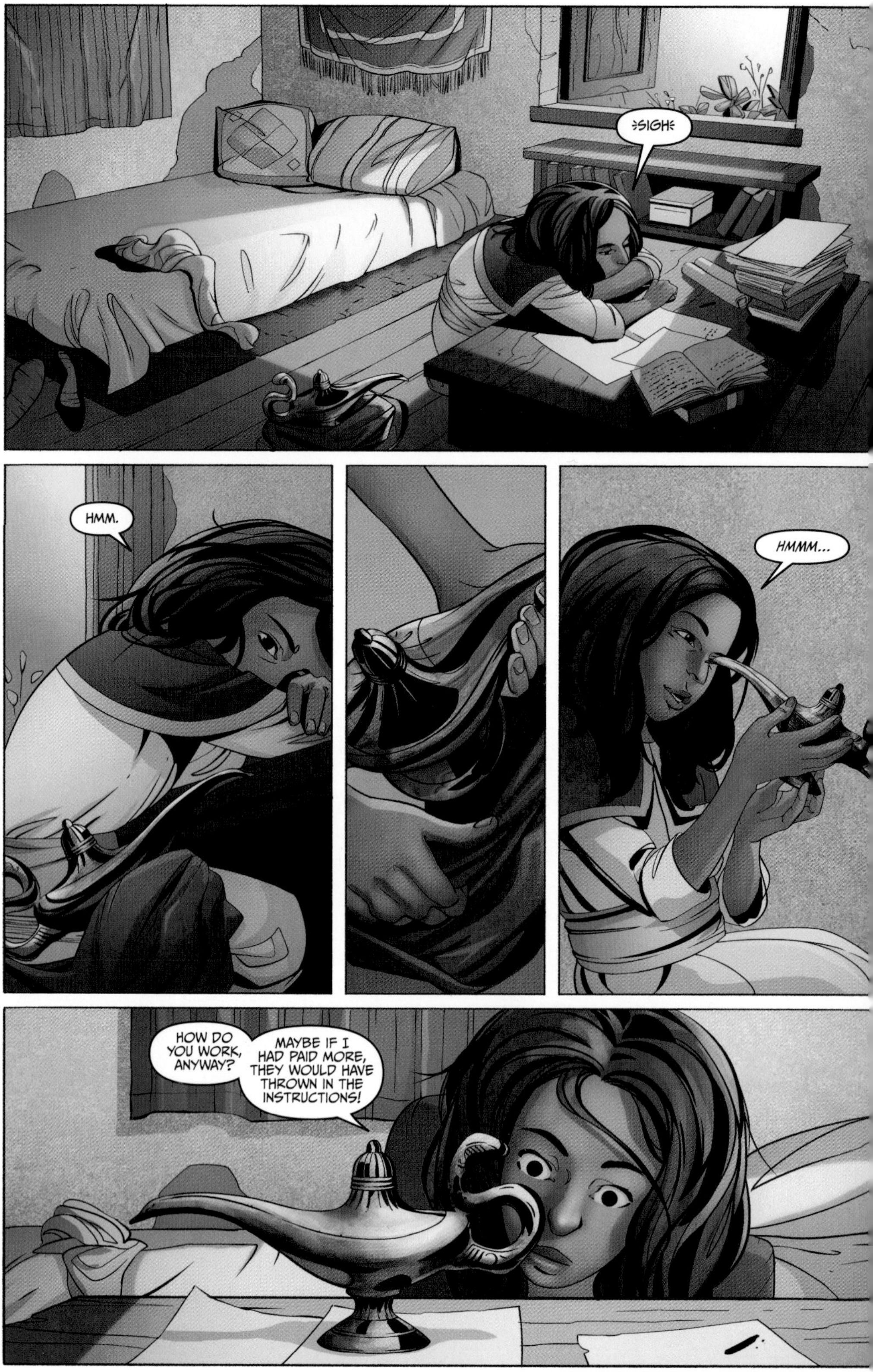

SIGH
HMM.
HMMM...
HOW DO YOU WORK, ANYWAY?
MAYBE IF I HAD PAID MORE, THEY WOULD HAVE THROWN IN THE INSTRUCTIONS!

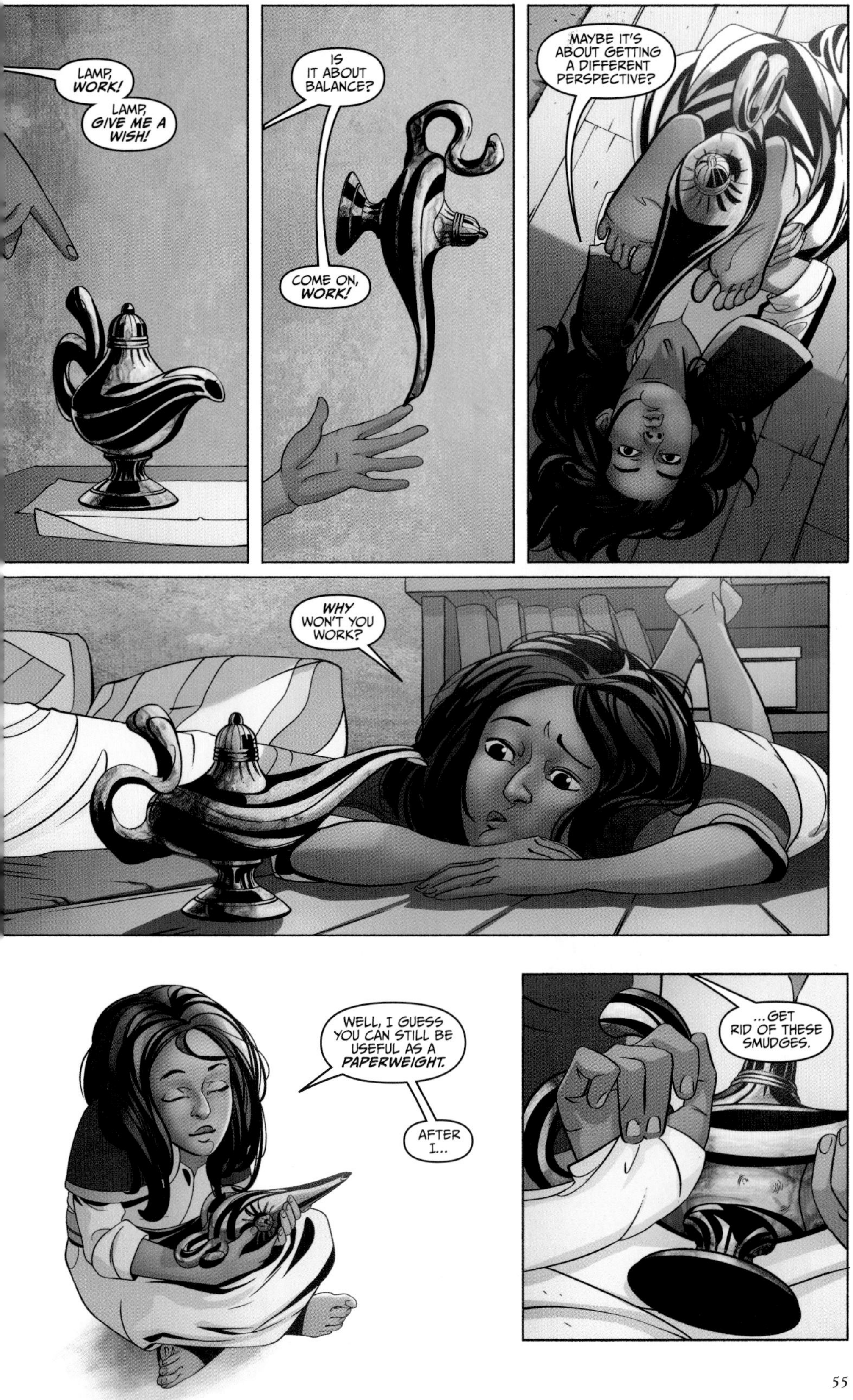
LAMP, WORK!
LAMP, GIVE ME A WISH!
IS IT ABOUT BALANCE?
COME ON, WORK!
MAYBE IT'S ABOUT GETTING A DIFFERENT PERSPECTIVE?
WHY WON'T YOU WORK?
WELL, I GUESS YOU CAN STILL BE USEFUL AS A PAPERWEIGHT.
AFTER I...
...GET RID OF THESE SMUDGES.

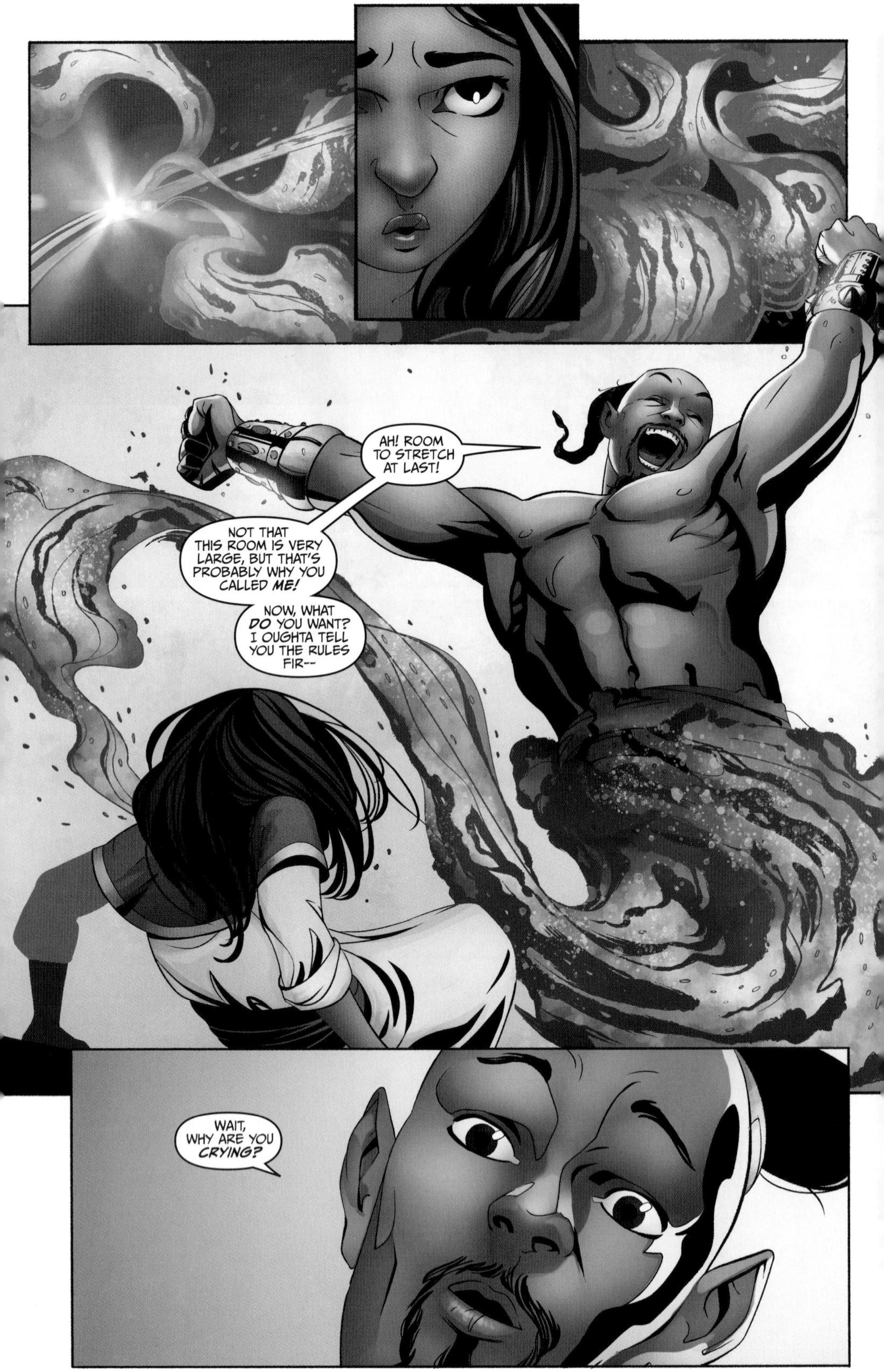
AH! ROOM TO STRETCH AT LAST!
NOT THAT THIS ROOM IS VERY LARGE, BUT THAT'S PROBABLY WHY YOU CALLED *ME!*
NOW, WHAT *DO* YOU WANT? I OUGHTA TELL YOU THE RULES FIR--
WAIT, WHY ARE YOU *CRYING?*

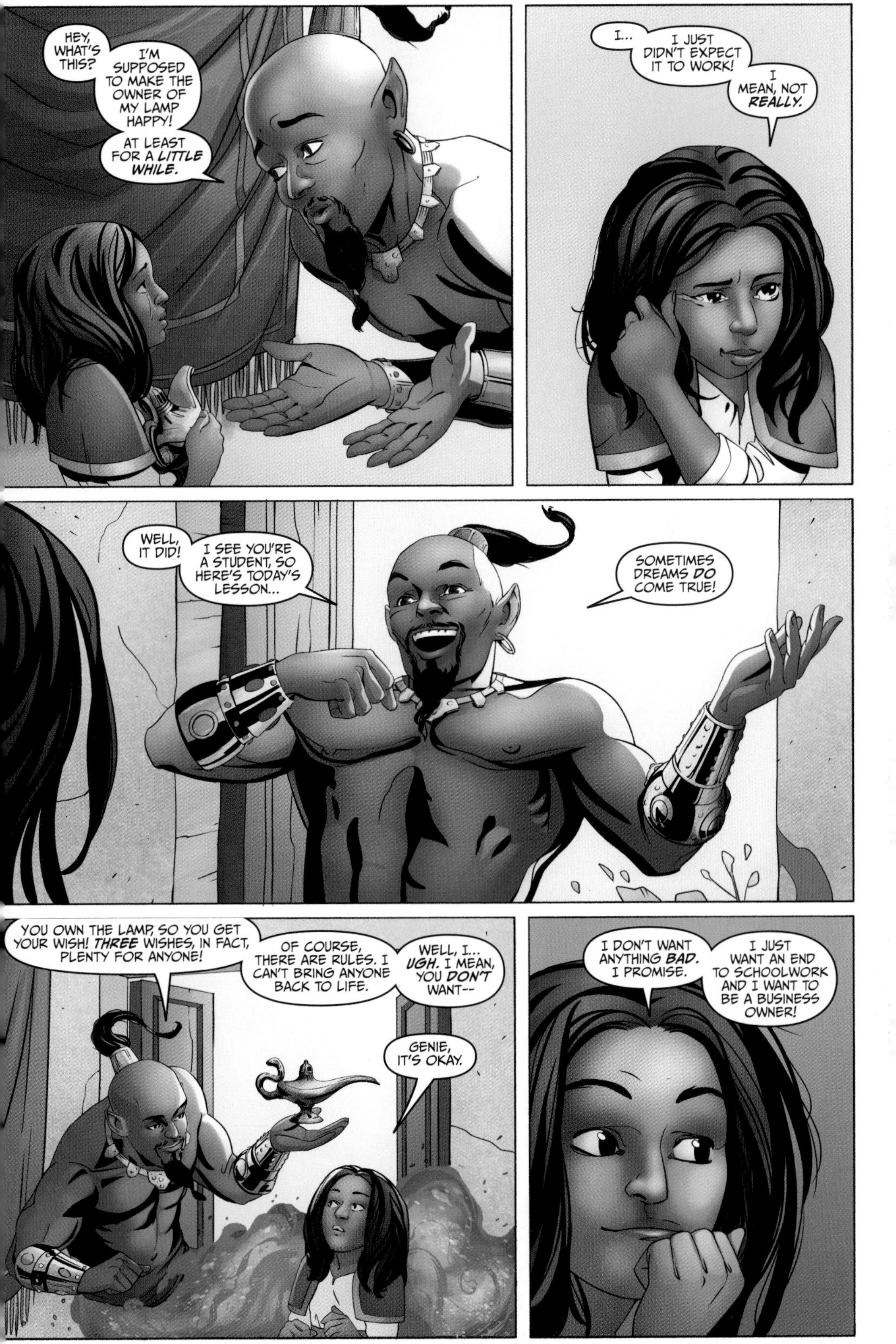
HEY, WHAT'S THIS?
I'M SUPPOSED TO MAKE THE OWNER OF MY LAMP HAPPY!
AT LEAST FOR A *LITTLE WHILE.*
I... I JUST DIDN'T EXPECT IT TO WORK!
I MEAN, NOT *REALLY.*
WELL, IT DID!
I SEE YOU'RE A STUDENT, SO HERE'S TODAY'S LESSON...
SOMETIMES DREAMS *DO* COME TRUE!
YOU OWN THE LAMP, SO YOU GET YOUR WISH! *THREE* WISHES, IN FACT, PLENTY FOR ANYONE!
OF COURSE, THERE ARE RULES. I CAN'T BRING ANYONE BACK TO LIFE.
WELL, I... *UGH.* I MEAN, YOU *DON'T* WANT--
GENIE, IT'S OKAY.
I DON'T WANT ANYTHING *BAD.* I PROMISE.
I JUST WANT AN END TO SCHOOLWORK AND I WANT TO BE A BUSINESS OWNER!

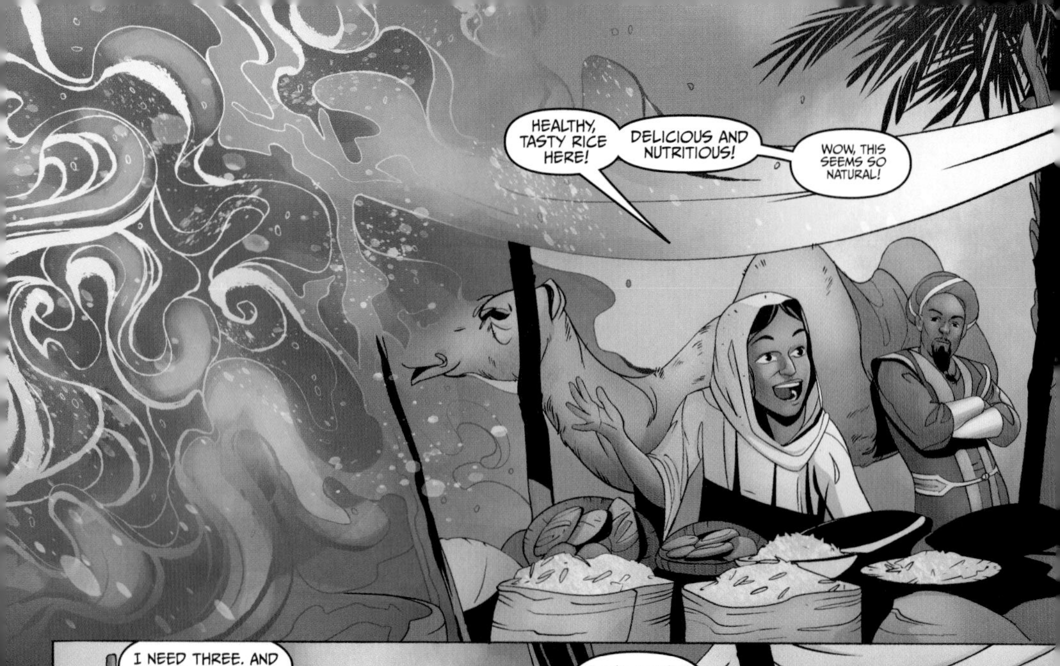
HEALTHY, TASTY RICE HERE!
DELICIOUS AND NUTRITIOUS!
WOW, THIS SEEMS SO NATURAL!

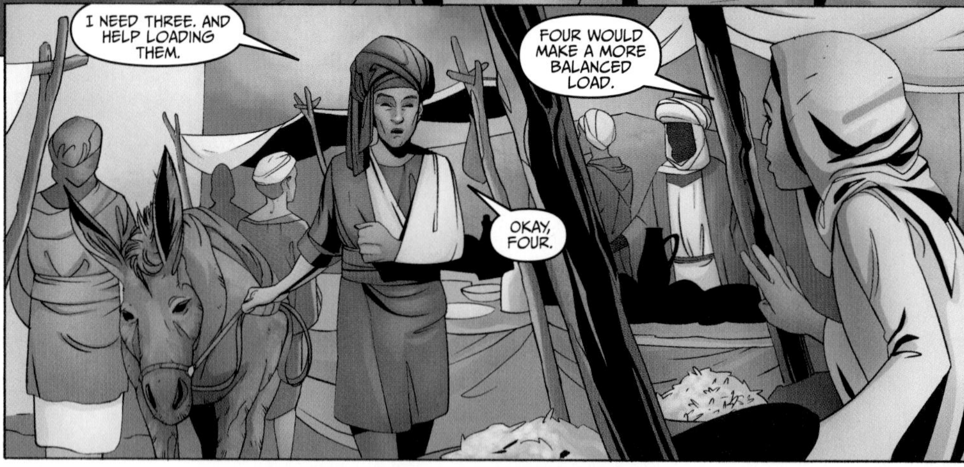
I NEED THREE. AND HELP LOADING THEM.
FOUR WOULD MAKE A MORE BALANCED LOAD.
OKAY, FOUR.

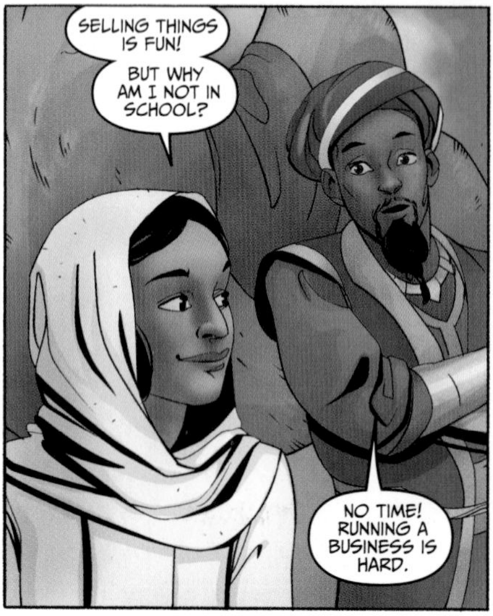
SELLING THINGS IS FUN!
BUT WHY AM I NOT IN SCHOOL?
NO TIME! RUNNING A BUSINESS IS HARD.

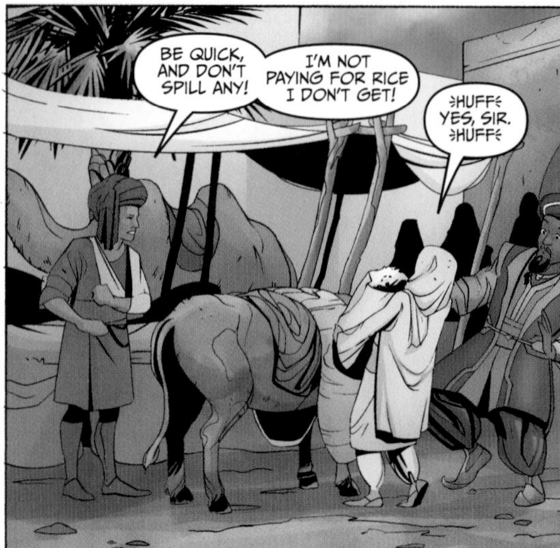
BE QUICK, AND DON'T SPILL ANY!
I'M NOT PAYING FOR RICE I DON'T GET!
HUFF YES, SIR. HUFF

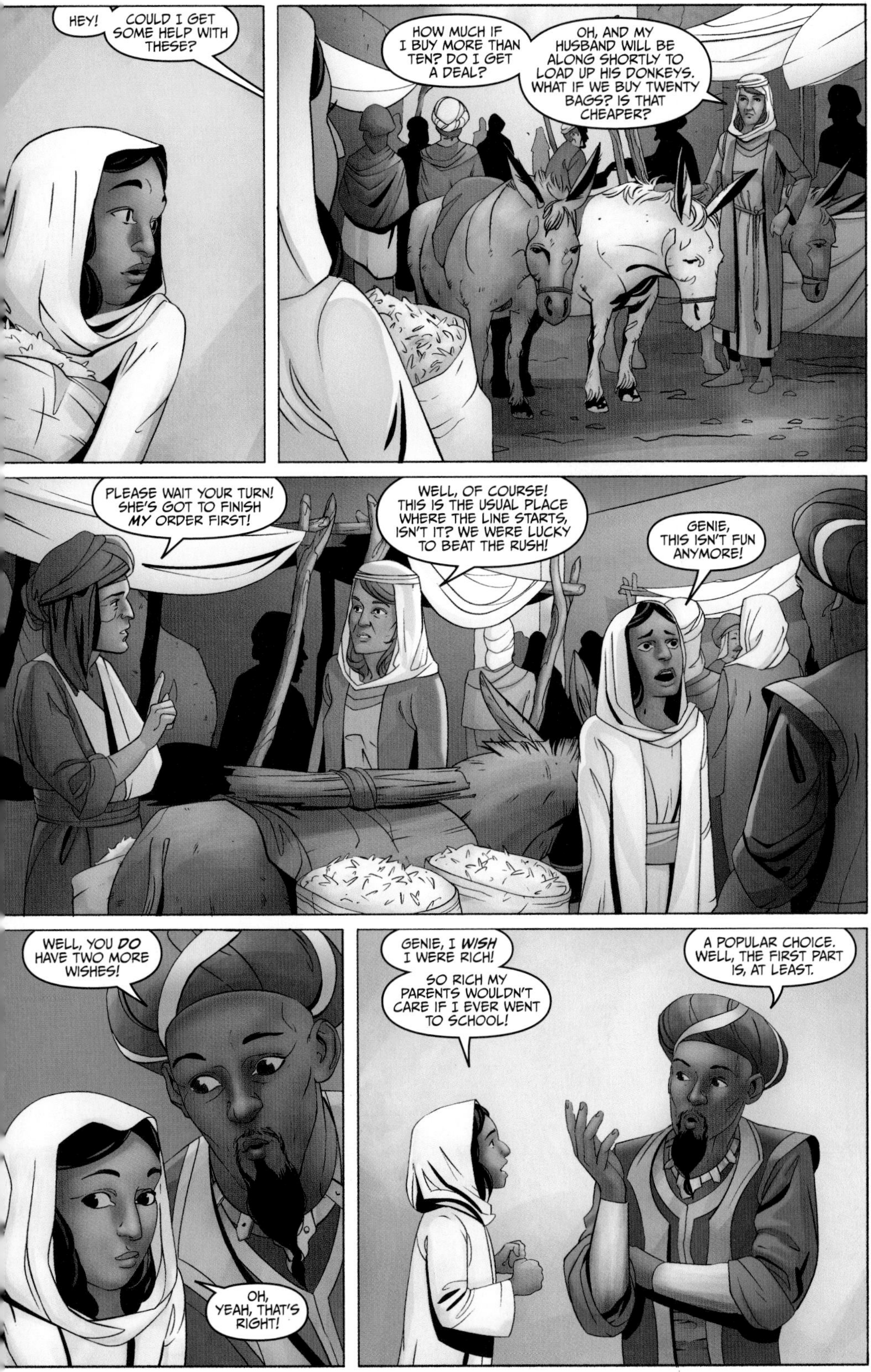
HEY!
COULD I GET SOME HELP WITH THESE?
HOW MUCH IF I BUY MORE THAN TEN? DO I GET A DEAL?
OH, AND MY HUSBAND WILL BE ALONG SHORTLY TO LOAD UP HIS DONKEYS. WHAT IF WE BUY TWENTY BAGS? IS THAT CHEAPER?
PLEASE WAIT YOUR TURN! SHE'S GOT TO FINISH *MY* ORDER FIRST!
WELL, OF COURSE! THIS IS THE USUAL PLACE WHERE THE LINE STARTS, ISN'T IT? WE WERE LUCKY TO BEAT THE RUSH!
GENIE, THIS ISN'T FUN ANYMORE!
WELL, YOU *DO* HAVE TWO MORE WISHES!
OH, YEAH, THAT'S RIGHT!
GENIE, I *WISH* I WERE RICH!
SO RICH MY PARENTS WOULDN'T CARE IF I EVER WENT TO SCHOOL!
A POPULAR CHOICE. WELL, THE FIRST PART IS, AT LEAST.

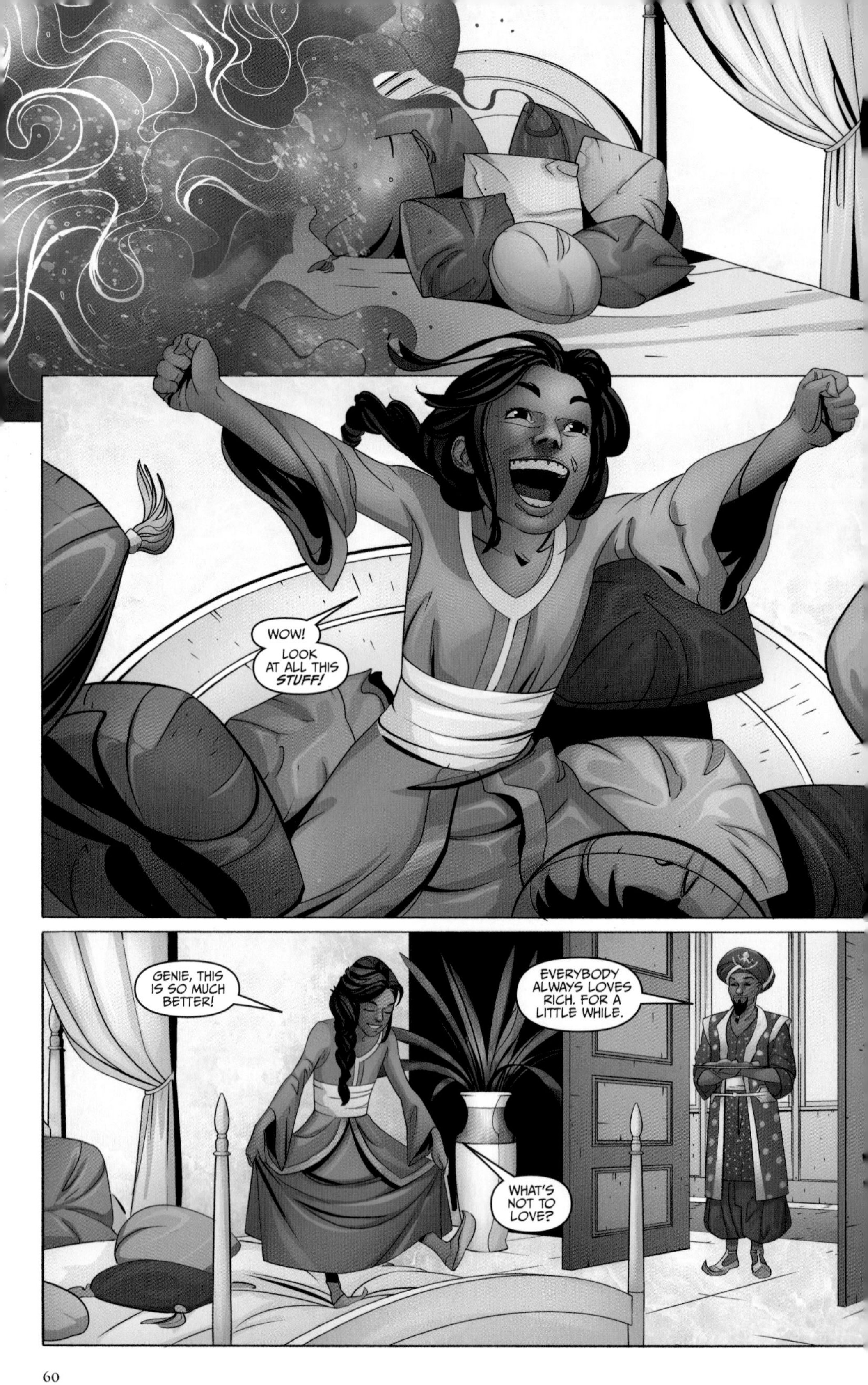
WOW!
LOOK AT ALL THIS STUFF!
GENIE, THIS IS SO MUCH BETTER!
EVERYBODY ALWAYS LOVES RICH. FOR A LITTLE WHILE.
WHAT'S NOT TO LOVE?

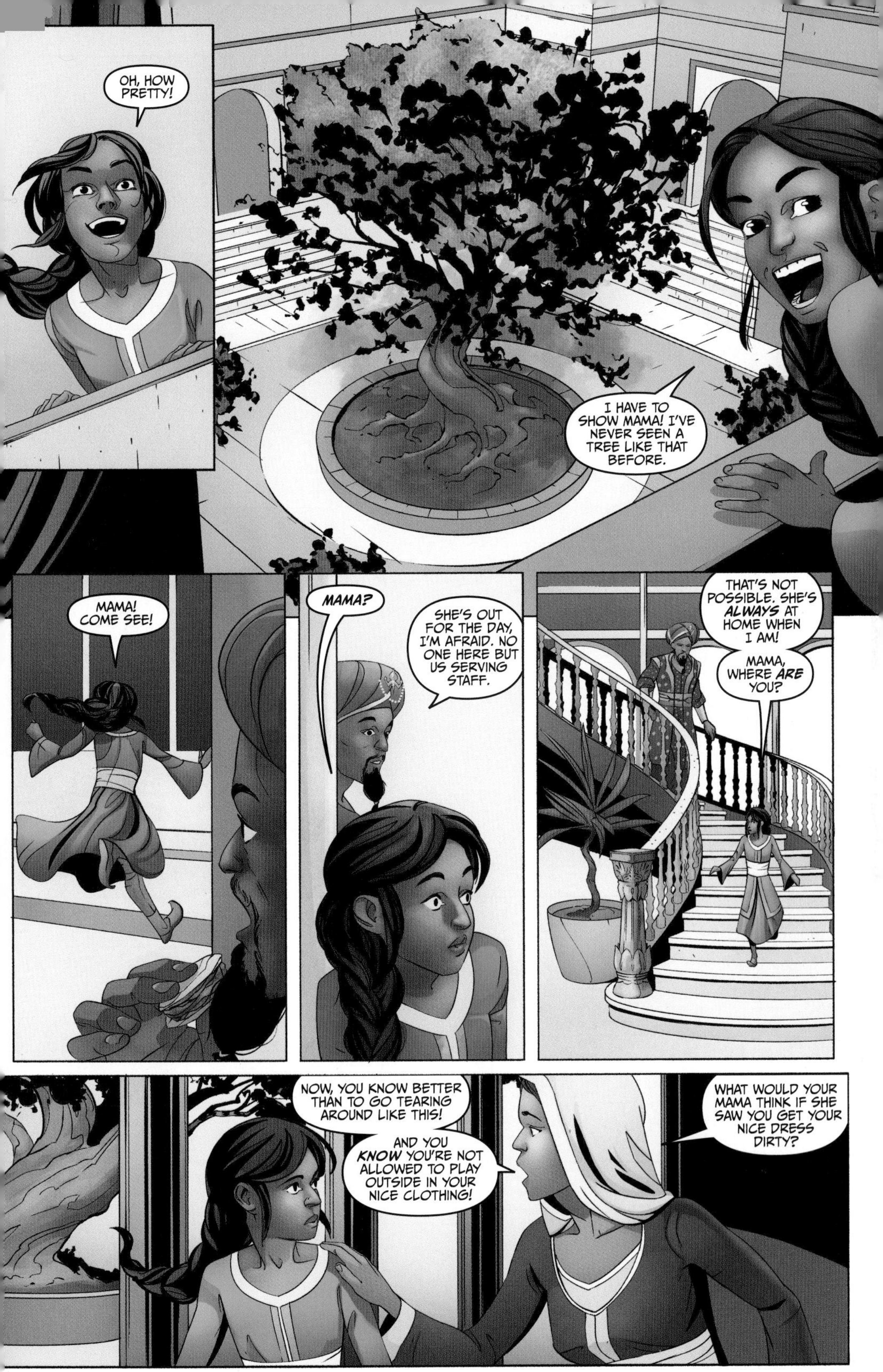
OH, HOW PRETTY!
I HAVE TO SHOW MAMA! I'VE NEVER SEEN A TREE LIKE THAT BEFORE.
MAMA! COME SEE!
MAMA?
SHE'S OUT FOR THE DAY, I'M AFRAID. NO ONE HERE BUT US SERVING STAFF.
THAT'S NOT POSSIBLE. SHE'S ALWAYS AT HOME WHEN I AM!
MAMA, WHERE ARE YOU?
NOW, YOU KNOW BETTER THAN TO GO TEARING AROUND LIKE THIS!
AND YOU KNOW YOU'RE NOT ALLOWED TO PLAY OUTSIDE IN YOUR NICE CLOTHING!
WHAT WOULD YOUR MAMA THINK IF SHE SAW YOU GET YOUR NICE DRESS DIRTY?

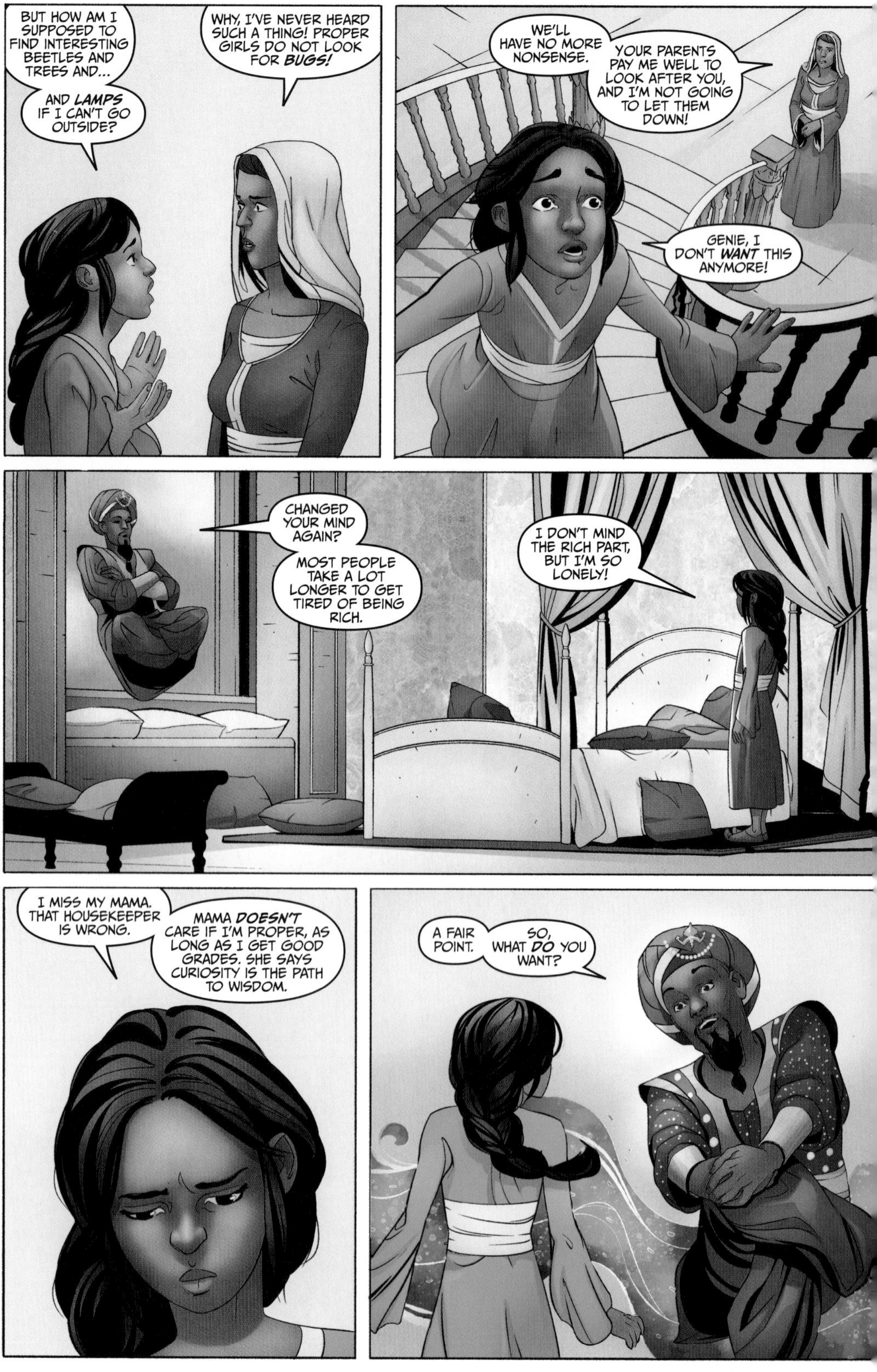
BUT HOW AM I SUPPOSED TO FIND INTERESTING BEETLES AND TREES AND...
AND LAMPS IF I CAN'T GO OUTSIDE?
WHY, I'VE NEVER HEARD SUCH A THING! PROPER GIRLS DO NOT LOOK FOR BUGS!
WE'LL HAVE NO MORE NONSENSE.
YOUR PARENTS PAY ME WELL TO LOOK AFTER YOU, AND I'M NOT GOING TO LET THEM DOWN!
GENIE, I DON'T WANT THIS ANYMORE!
CHANGED YOUR MIND AGAIN?
MOST PEOPLE TAKE A LOT LONGER TO GET TIRED OF BEING RICH.
I DON'T MIND THE RICH PART, BUT I'M SO LONELY!
I MISS MY MAMA. THAT HOUSEKEEPER IS WRONG.
MAMA DOESN'T CARE IF I'M PROPER, AS LONG AS I GET GOOD GRADES. SHE SAYS CURIOSITY IS THE PATH TO WISDOM.
A FAIR POINT.
SO, WHAT DO YOU WANT?

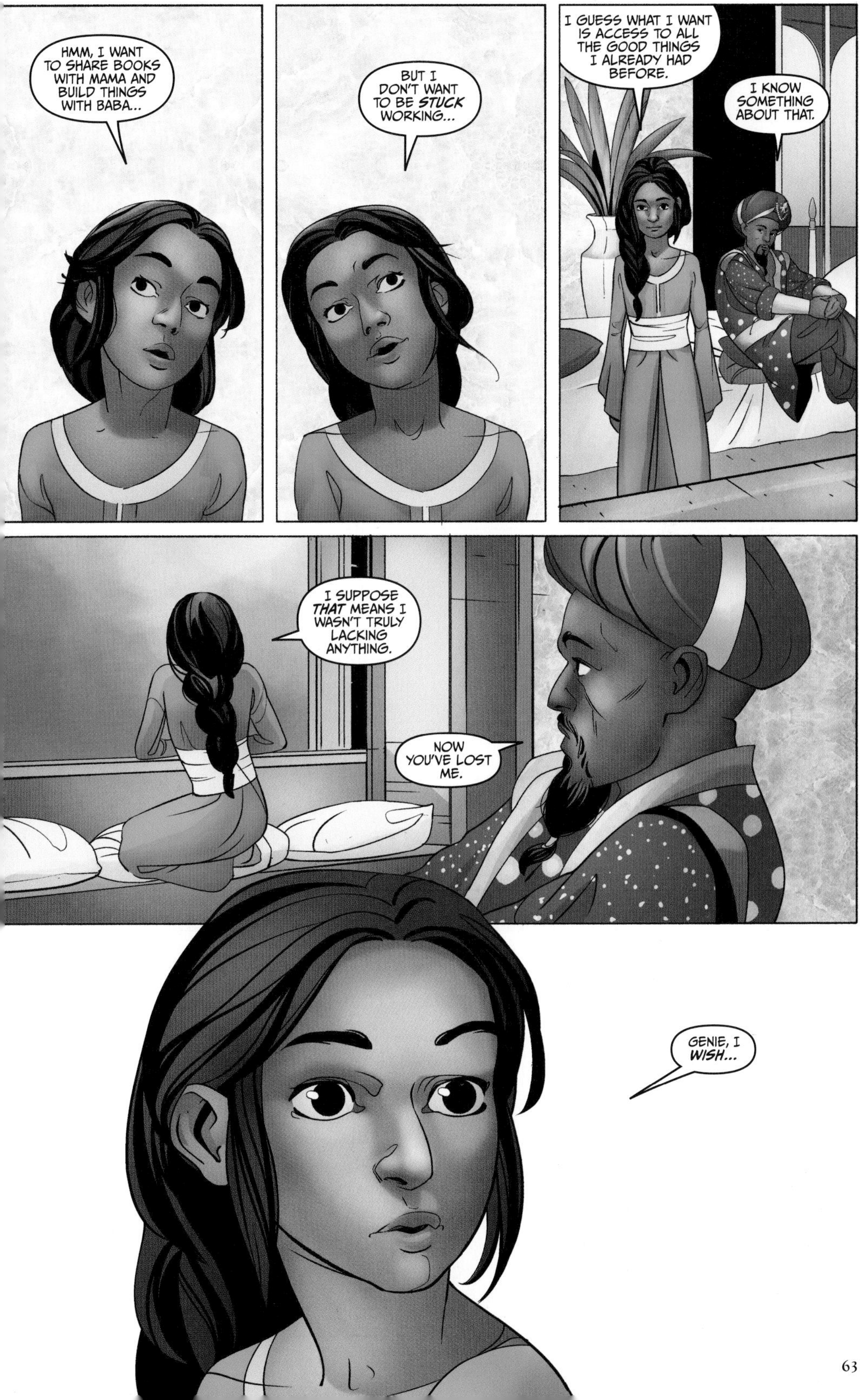
HMM, I WANT TO SHARE BOOKS WITH MAMA AND BUILD THINGS WITH BABA...
BUT I DON'T WANT TO BE STUCK WORKING...
I GUESS WHAT I WANT IS ACCESS TO ALL THE GOOD THINGS I ALREADY HAD BEFORE.
I KNOW SOMETHING ABOUT THAT.
I SUPPOSE THAT MEANS I WASN'T TRULY LACKING ANYTHING.
NOW YOU'VE LOST ME.
GENIE, I WISH...

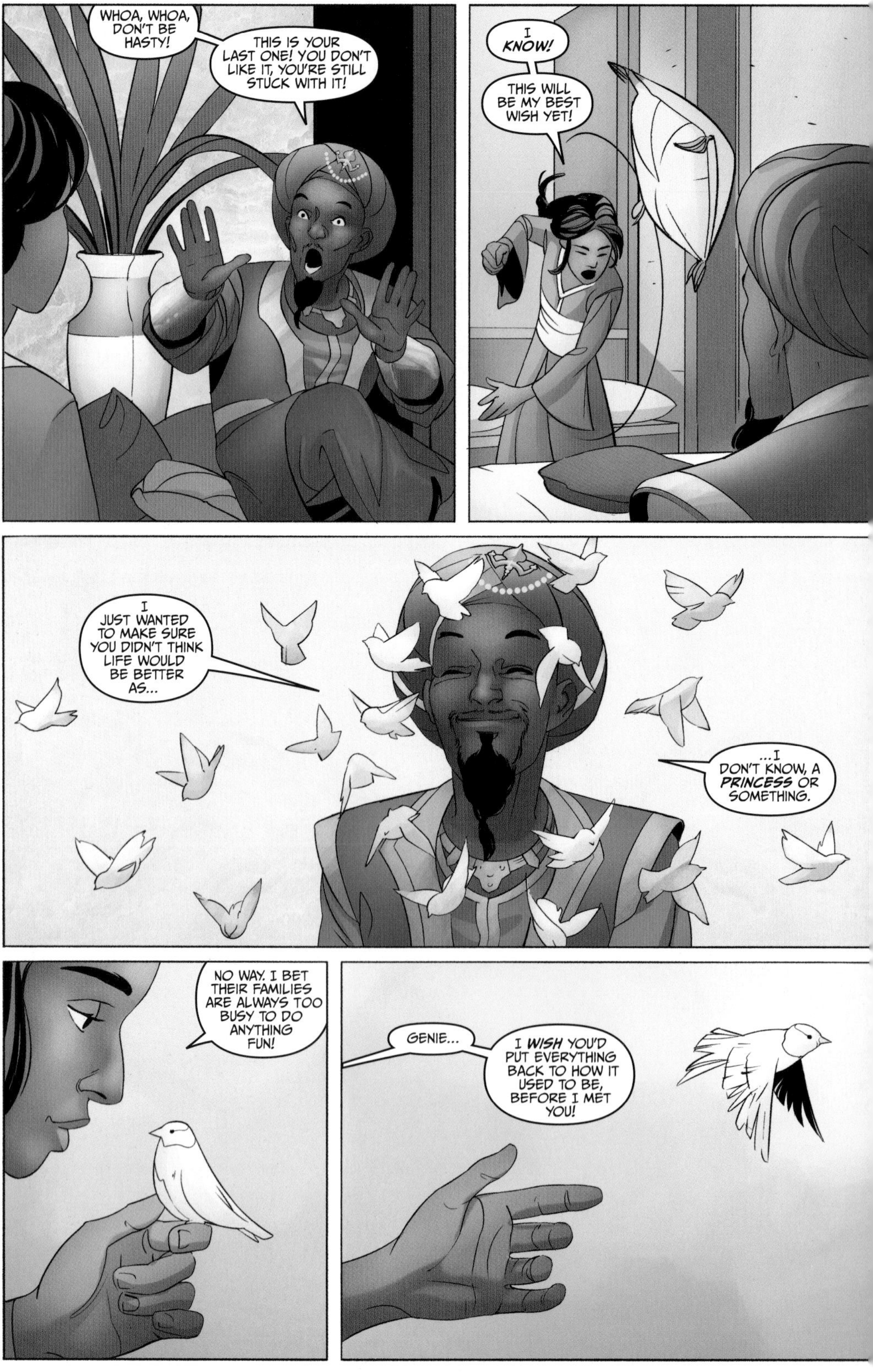
WHOA, WHOA, DON'T BE HASTY!
THIS IS YOUR LAST ONE! YOU DON'T LIKE IT, YOU'RE STILL STUCK WITH IT!
I KNOW!
THIS WILL BE MY BEST WISH YET!
I JUST WANTED TO MAKE SURE YOU DIDN'T THINK LIFE WOULD BE BETTER AS...
...I DON'T KNOW, A PRINCESS OR SOMETHING.
NO WAY. I BET THEIR FAMILIES ARE ALWAYS TOO BUSY TO DO ANYTHING FUN!
GENIE...
I WISH YOU'D PUT EVERYTHING BACK TO HOW IT USED TO BE, BEFORE I MET YOU!

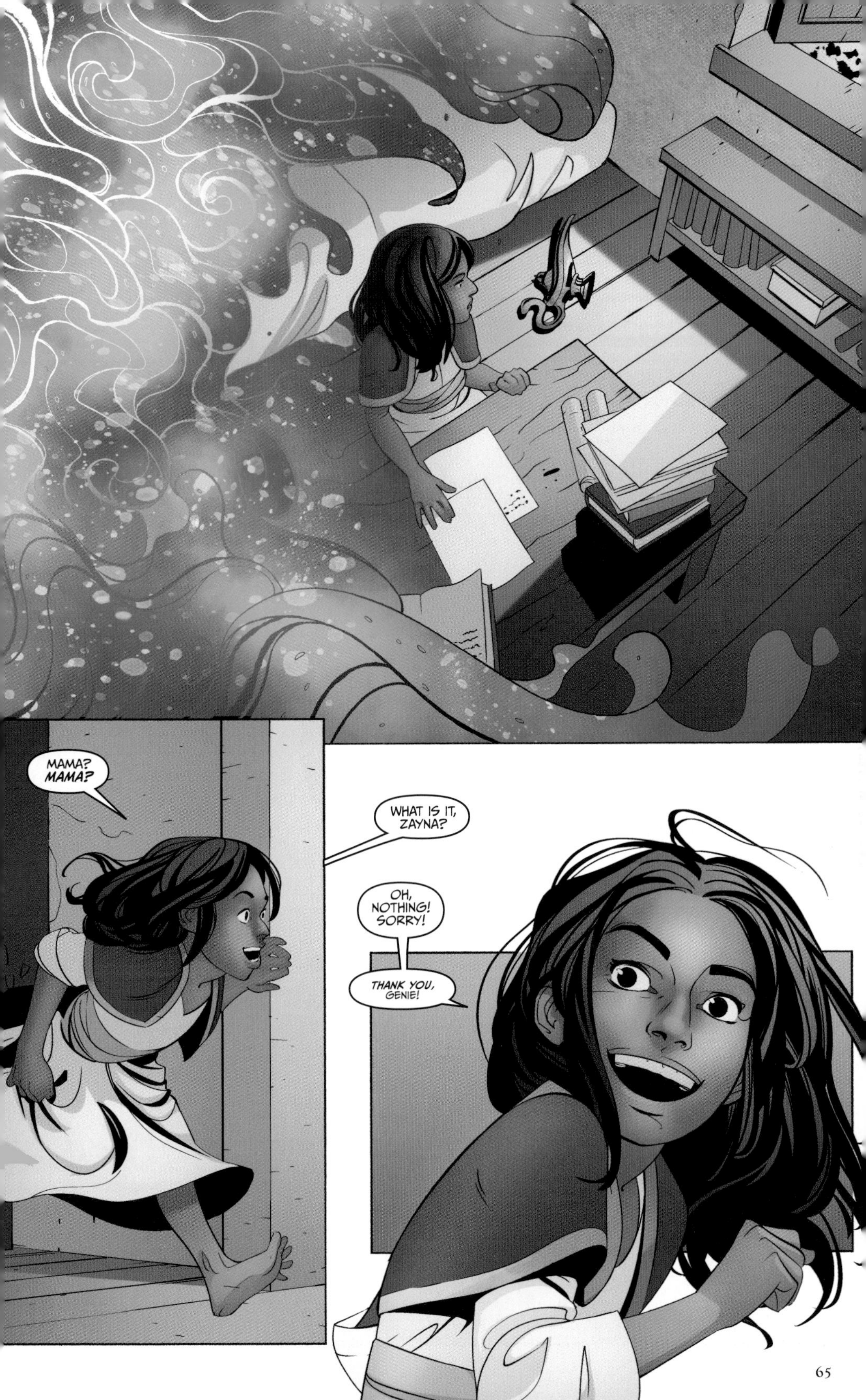
MAMA? MAMA?
WHAT IS IT, ZAYNA?
OH, NOTHING! SORRY!
THANK YOU, GENIE!

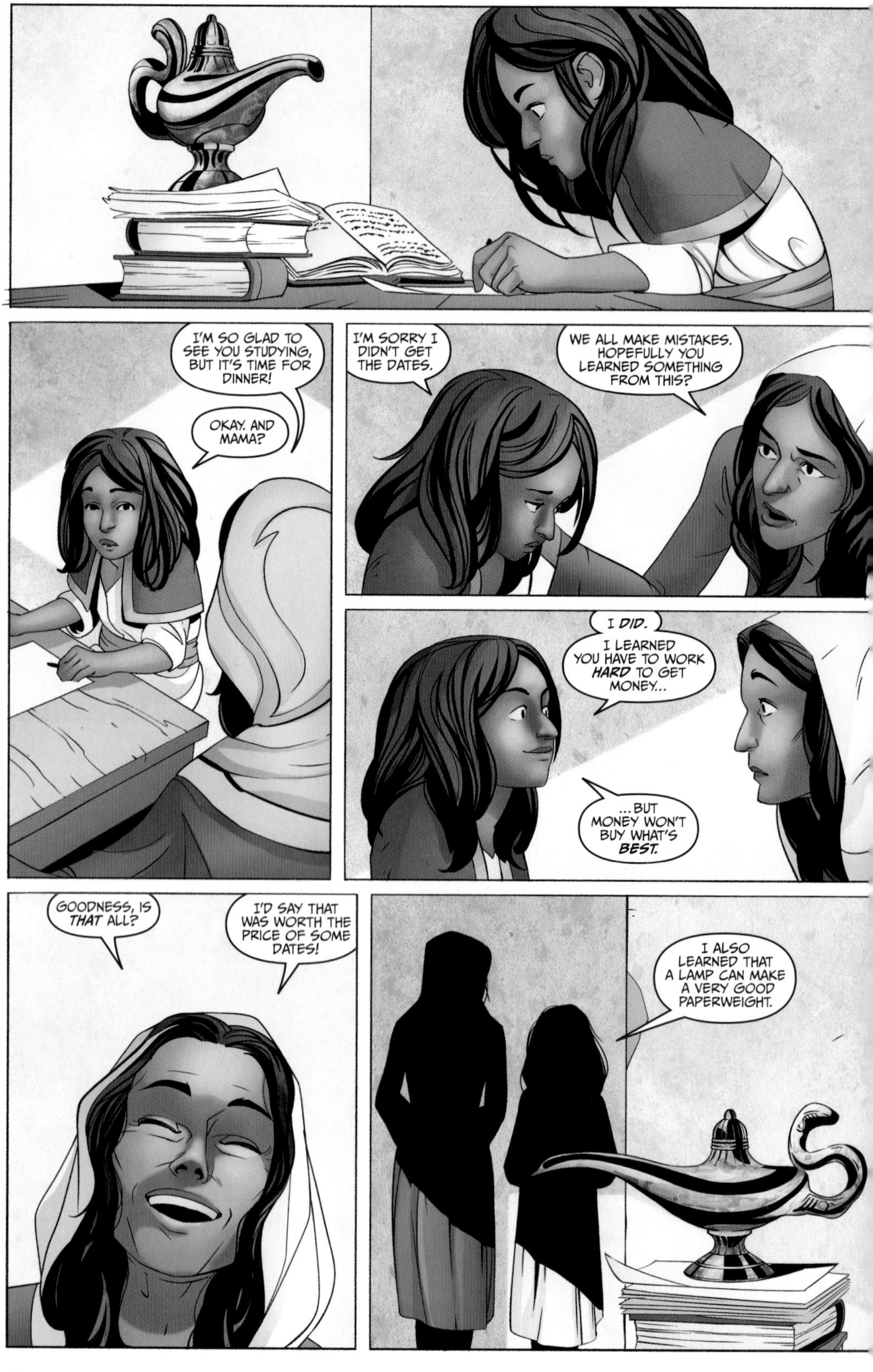
I'M SO GLAD TO SEE YOU STUDYING, BUT IT'S TIME FOR DINNER!
OKAY. AND MAMA?
I'M SORRY I DIDN'T GET THE DATES.
WE ALL MAKE MISTAKES. HOPEFULLY YOU LEARNED SOMETHING FROM THIS?
I *DID.*
I LEARNED YOU HAVE TO WORK **HARD** TO GET MONEY...
...BUT MONEY WON'T BUY WHAT'S **BEST.**
GOODNESS, IS *THAT* ALL?
I'D SAY THAT WAS WORTH THE PRICE OF SOME DATES!
I ALSO LEARNED THAT A LAMP CAN MAKE A VERY GOOD PAPERWEIGHT.

Four Tales of Agrabah
Sketchbook

Abu and Raja designs by Lalit Kumar Sharma.

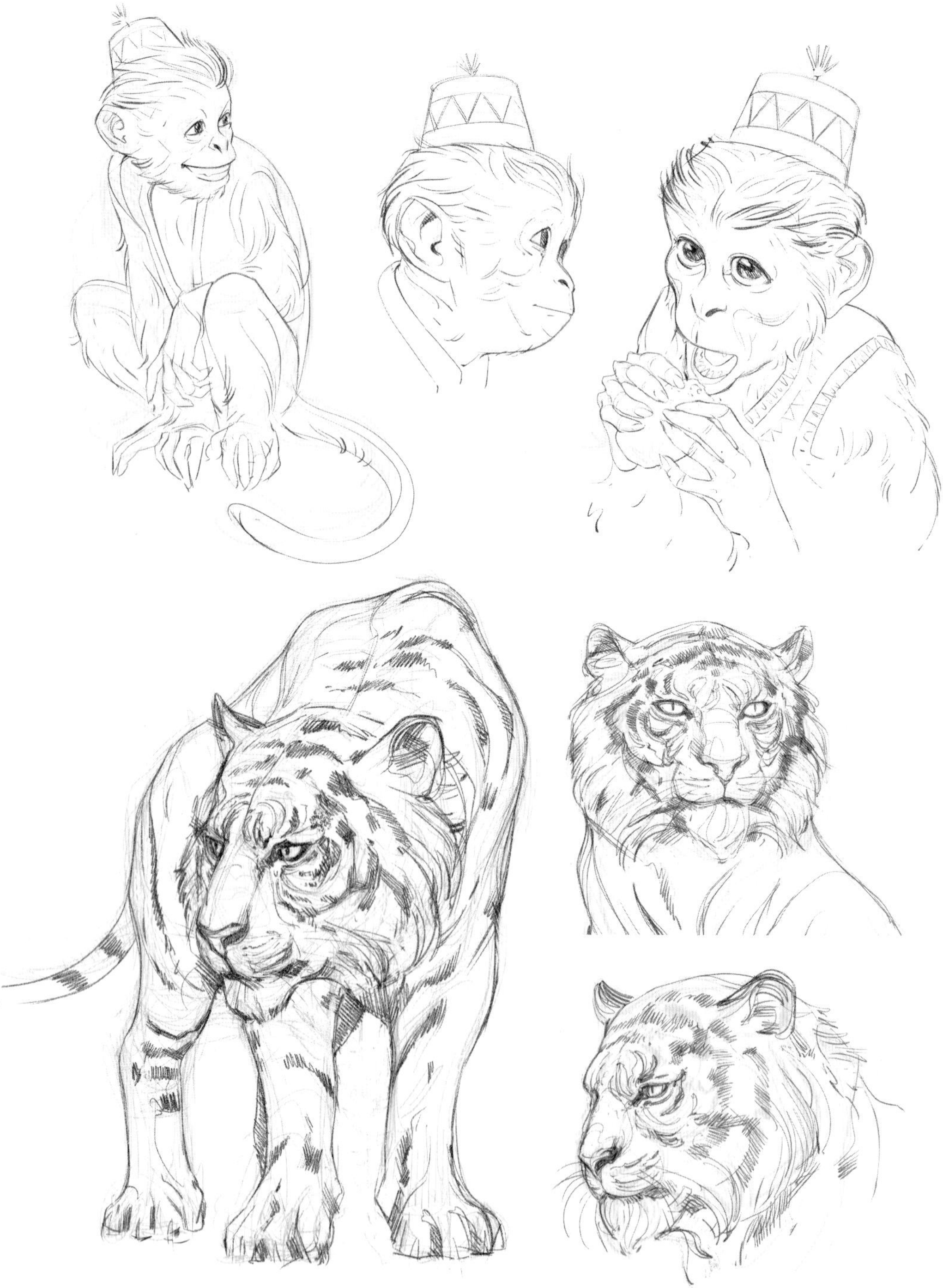

Abu and Raja designs by Pablo Andrés.

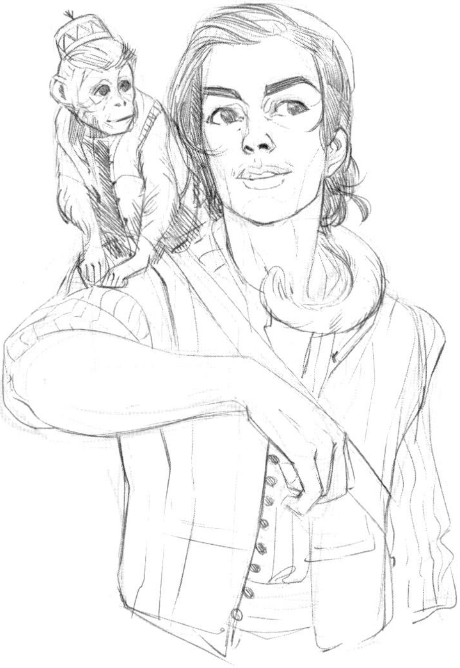

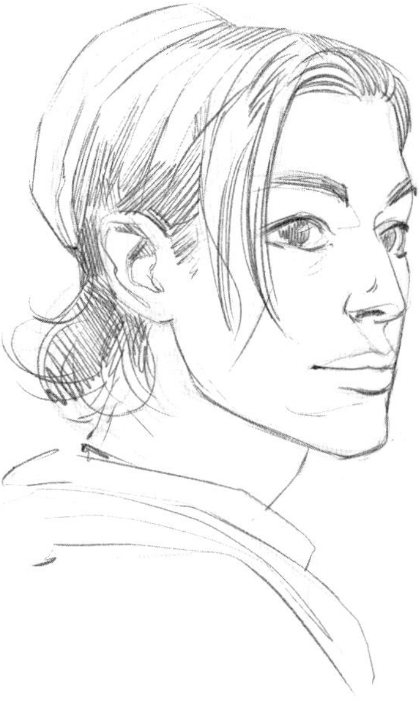

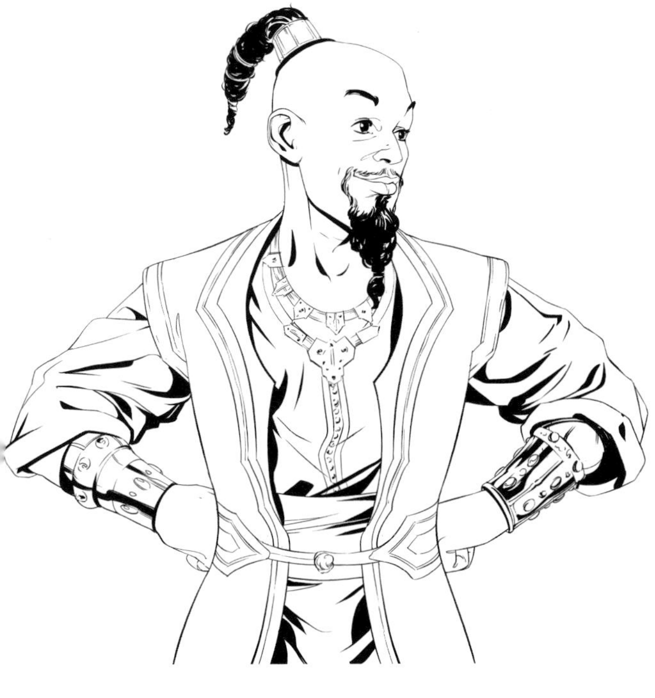

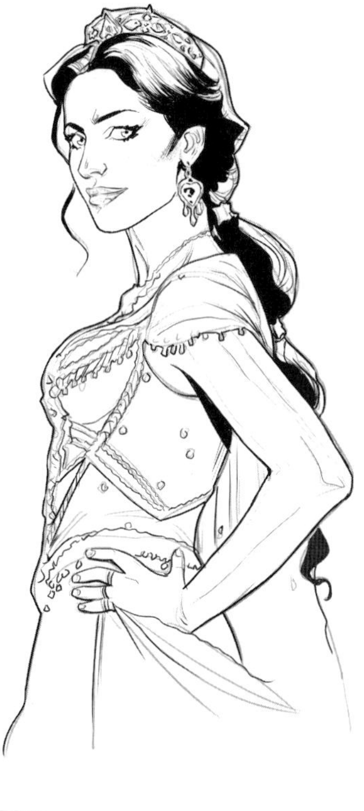

Aladdin and Genie character sketches by Pablo Andrés.
Jasmine character sketch by Diego Pérez Galindo.

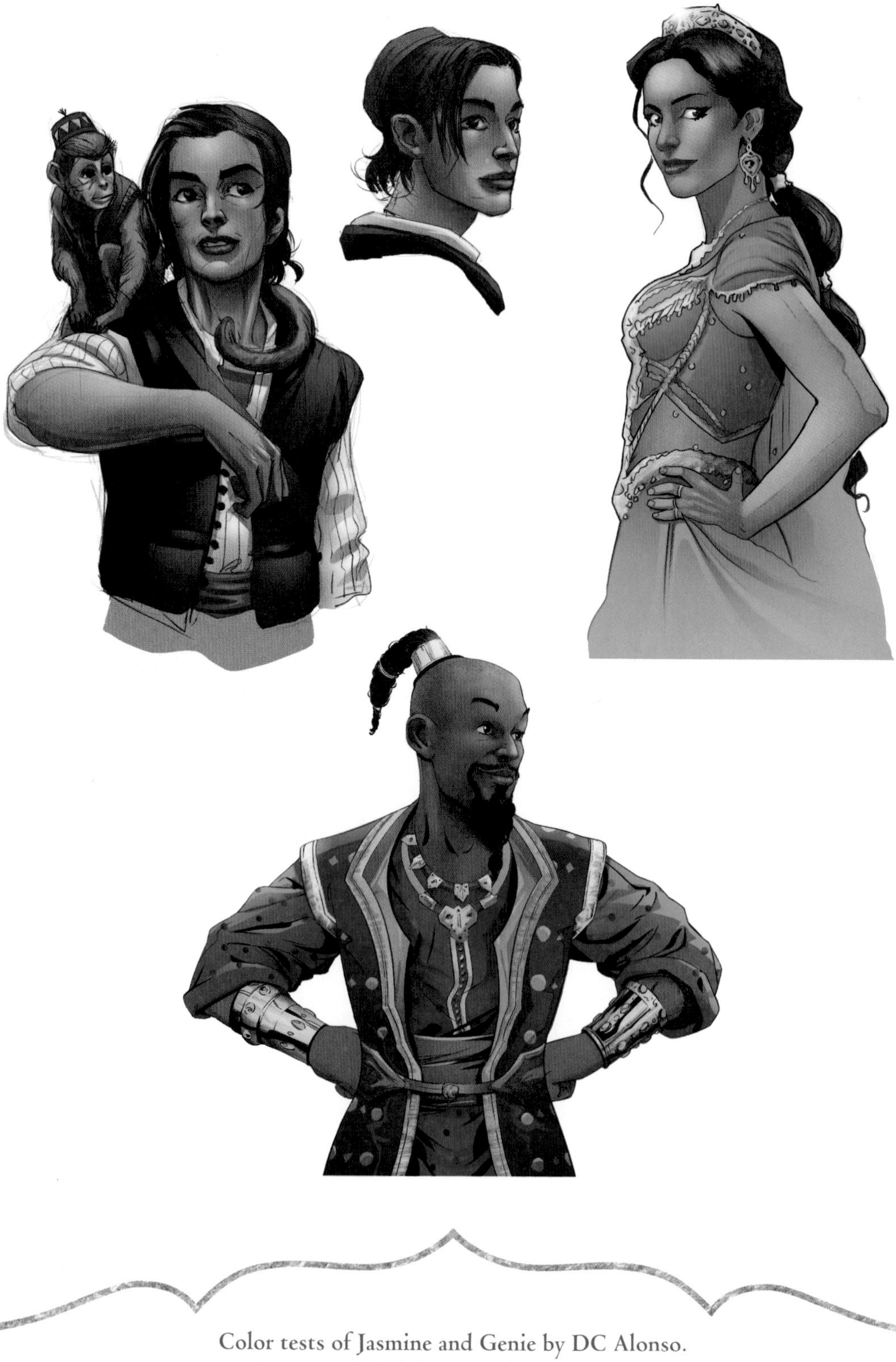

Color tests of Jasmine and Genie by DC Alonso.
Color test of Aladdin by Jordi Escuin Llorach.

Disney

CLASSIC STORIES RETOLD
WITH THE MAGIC OF DISNEY!

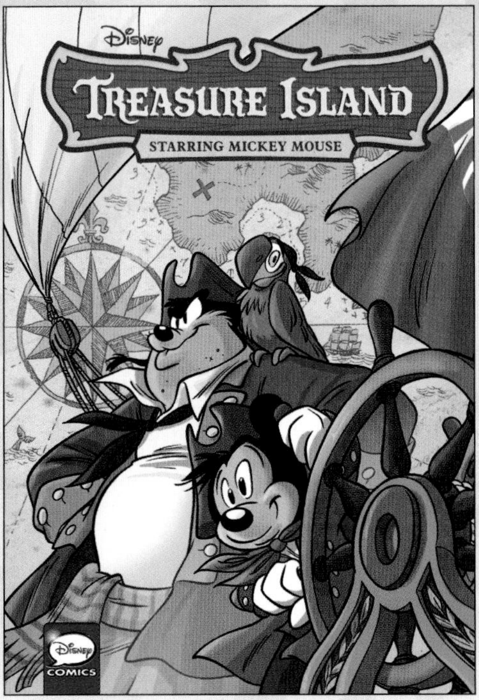
Disney
TREASURE ISLAND
STARRING MICKEY MOUSE
Disney
COMICS

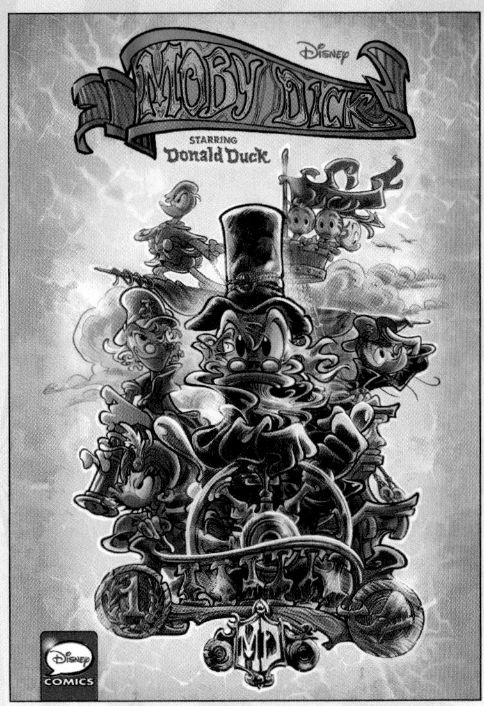
Disney
MOBY DICK
STARRING
Donald Duck
Disney
COMICS

Disney Treasure Island, starring Mickey Mouse

Robert Louis Stevenson's classic tale of pirates, treasure, and swashbuckling adventure comes to life in this adaptation that stars Mickey, Goofy, and Pegleg Pete! When Jim Mousekins discovers a map to buried treasure, his dream of adventure is realized with a voyage on the high seas, a quest through tropical island jungles . . . and a race to evade cutthroat pirates!

978-1-50671-158-4 ✠ $10.99

Disney Moby Dick, starring Donald Duck

In an adaptation of Herman Melville's classic, Scrooge McDuck, Donald, and nephews venture out on the high seas in pursuit of the white whale Moby Dick who stole Captain Quackhab's lucky dime. As Quackhab scours the ocean in pursuit of his nemesis, facing other dangers of the sea, the crew begin to wonder: how far will their captain go for revenge?

978-1-50671-157-7 ✠ $10.99

DARK HORSE BOOKS

AVAILABLE AT YOUR LOCAL COMICS SHOP OR BOOKSTORE! To find a comics shop in your area, visit comicshoplocator.com. For more information or to order direct: ✠ On the web: DarkHorse.com ✠ Email: mailorder@darkhorse.com ✠ Phone: 1-800-862-0052 Mon.–Fri. 9 a.m. to 5 p.m. Pacific Time

Disney COMICS

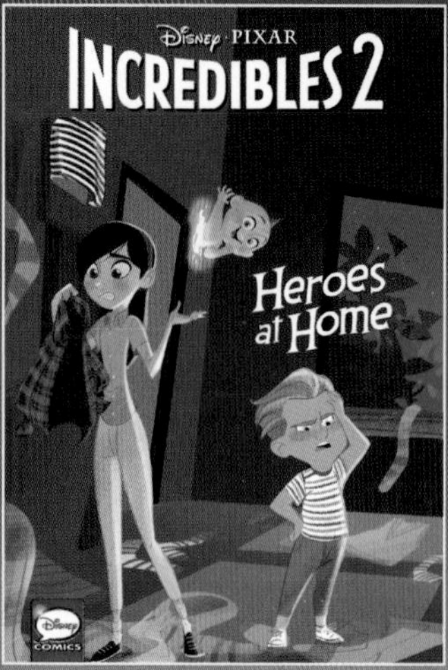
Disney · PIXAR
INCREDIBLES 2
Heroes at Home
Disney COMICS

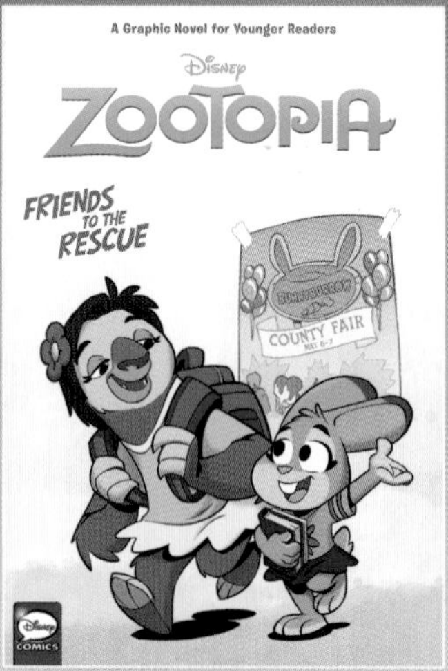
A Graphic Novel for Younger Readers
Disney
ZOOTOPIA
FRIENDS TO THE RESCUE
COUNTY FAIR
Disney COMICS

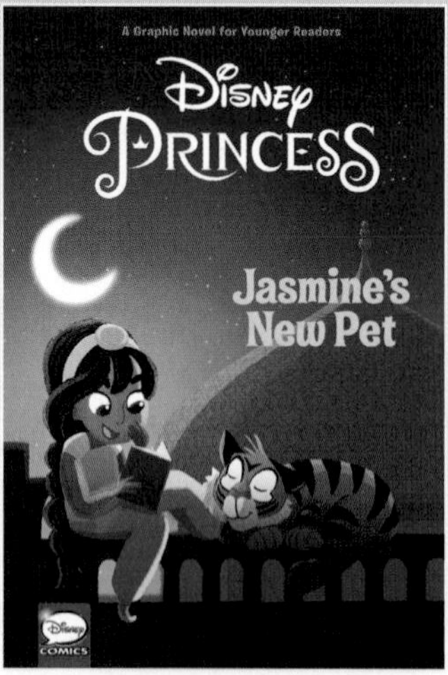
A Graphic Novel for Younger Readers
Disney
PRINCESS
Jasmine's New Pet
Disney COMICS

LOOKING FOR BOOKS FOR YOUNGER READERS?

$7.99 each!

EACH VOLUME INCLUDES A SECTION OF FUN ACTIVITIES!

DISNEY·PIXAR INCREDIBLES 2: HEROES AT HOME

Violet and Dash are part of a Super family, and they are trying to help out at home. Can they pick up groceries and secretly stop some bad guys? And then can they clean up the house while Jack-Jack is "sleeping"?

ISBN 978-1-50670-943-7 | $7.99

DISNEY ZOOTOPIA: FRIENDS TO THE RESCUE

Young Judy Hopps proves she's a brave little bunny when she helps a classmate. And can a quick-thinking young Nick Wilde liven up a birthday party? Friends save the day in these tales of Zootopia!

ISBN 978-1-50671-054-9 | $7.99

DISNEY PRINCESS: JASMINE'S NEW PET

Jasmine has a new pet tiger, Rajah, but he's not quite ready for palace life. Will she be able to train the young cub before the Sultan finds him another home?

ISBN 978-1-50671-052-5 | $7.99

AVAILABLE AT YOUR LOCAL COMICS SHOP OR BOOKSTORE! TO FIND A COMICS SHOP IN YOUR AREA, VISIT COMICSHOPLOCATOR.COM

For more information or to order direct: On the web: DarkHorse.com | Email: mailorder@darkhorse.com
Phone: 1-800-862-0052 Mon.–Fri. 9 a.m. to 5 p.m. Pacific Time